He foun[d] [her by the]
fireplace. He'd never seen anything
more lovely, more perfect in his life.

He took a step closer to her. She took a step toward him. Then another, and another.

"What are we doing?" she whispered.

The closer they got, the less sense any of this made. "I don't know."

"This probably isn't a good idea."

He closed the distance between them. "Probably not."

One taste. That was all he wanted.

Stop.

Logically that was what he should do, but Gabe was beyond rational thought and action. Everything he'd been searching for his entire life was suddenly right here in his arms. He hadn't felt this way in years. Not since his ex-wife, Lana.

And then reality hit like a wrecking ball.

Faith wouldn't be sticking around, either.

Dear Reader,

What does romance mean to you? Sure, it could be sharing a candlelit dinner or strolling hand in hand on a spring day. But to me it's even the smallest of gestures that tells you the person you think hangs the sun and the moon finds you equally unforgettable. As a lifelong romantic who met her future husband nearly twenty years ago, I'm delighted to be heading up Silhouette Romance. These books remind me that no matter what challenges the day has held, finding true love is one of life's greatest rewards.

Bestselling author Judy Christenberry kicks off another great month with *Finding a Family* (SR #1762). In this sweet romance, a down-to-earth cowboy goes "shopping" for the perfect woman for his father but instead finds himself the target of Cupid's arrow! Watch the sparks fly in Melissa McClone's *Blueprint for a Wedding* (SR #1763) when a man who has crafted the perfect blueprint for domestic bliss finds himself attracted to an actress who doesn't believe in happy endings. This month's "Cinderella" is a feisty Latina, as Angie Ray continues Silhouette Romance's commitment to offering modern-day fairy tales in *The Millionaire's Reward* (SR #1764). Part of the SOULMATES series, *Moonlight Magic* (SR #1765) by Doris Rangel features a vacationing nurse who falls for a handsome stranger with a particularly vexing habit of vanishing into thin air.

And be sure to stay tuned for next month's exciting lineup when reader favorites Raye Morgan and Carol Grace return with two classic romances.

Ann Leslie Tuttle
Associate Senior Editor

Please address questions and book requests to:
Silhouette Reader Service
U.S.: 3010 Walden Ave., P.O. Box 1325, Buffalo, NY 14269
Canadian: P.O. Box 609, Fort Erie, Ont. L2A 5X3

Blueprint for a Wedding

MELISSA McCLONE

SILHOUETTE *Romance*®

Published by Silhouette Books

America's Publisher of Contemporary Romance

For my family

Special thanks to John Gustafson at Beals Design/Build
and Margaret Buchan at the Green Gables Inn for
answering all my questions, and to Betsy Eliot and
Virginia Kantra for keeping me going.

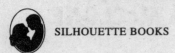 SILHOUETTE BOOKS

ISBN 0-373-19763-2

BLUEPRINT FOR A WEDDING

Visit Silhouette Books at www.eHarlequin.com

Printed in U.S.A.

Books by Melissa McClone

Silhouette Romance

If the Ring Fits... #1431
*The Wedding Lullaby #1485
His Band of Gold #1537
In Deep Waters #1608
*The Wedding Adventure #1661
Santa Brought a Son #1698
*The Billionaire's Wedding Masquerade #1740
*Blueprint for a Wedding #1763

Yours Truly

Fiancé for the Night

*Matches by Henry

MELISSA McCLONE

With a degree in mechanical engineering from Stanford University, the last thing Melissa McClone ever thought she would be doing is writing romance novels, but analyzing engines for a major U.S. airline just couldn't compete with her "happily-ever-afters."

When she isn't writing, caring for her three young children or doing laundry, Melissa loves to curl up on the couch with a cup of tea, her cats and a good book. She enjoys watching home decorating shows to get ideas for her house—a 1939 cottage that is *slowly* being renovated.

Melissa lives in Lake Oswego, Oregon, with her own real-life hero husband, two daughters, a son, two lovable but oh-so-spoiled indoor cats and a no-longer-stray outdoor kitty who decided to call the garage home. Melissa loves to hear from readers. You can write to her at P.O. Box 63, Lake Oswego, OR 97034.

Henry Davenport's Matchmaking List

<u>Friends</u>   <u>Possible Match</u>

Brett Matthews   Laurel Worthington

Married with one child!
(*The Wedding Lullaby;* SR #1485)

Cynthia Sterling   Cade Armstrong Waters

Engaged!
(*The Wedding Adventure;* SR #1661)

Henry Davenport   Elisabeth Wheeler

A match made by his conniving friends!
(*The Billionaire's Wedding Masquerade;* SR #1740)

Gabriel Logan   Faith Starr Addison

Only time will tell,
but it's looking promising so far!

Prologue

From the latest edition of *Weekly Secrets:*

Losing Faith?
by Garrett Malloy and Fred Silvers

The lovely and talented film actress Faith Starr is calling it quits. With a string of five broken engagements, one might expect the Golden Globe nominee to be tossing out yet another fiancé with yesterday's trash. But *Weekly Secrets* has learned the stunning Faith is not leaving a man, but—prepare yourselves faithful fans—acting.

Despite the lackluster box-office performance of her last two films and rumors surrounding the release of her upcoming movie, *Jupiter Tears,* a $150-million space epic still in postproduction after two canceled premiere dates, studio heads have been campaigning to woo her back.

But the A-list leading lady is not returning phone calls. Neither her manager nor publicist will comment.

Perhaps Faith needs a vacation from the spotlight following her latest and most public breakup with *Jupiter Tears* costar and heartthrob, Rio Rivers. This on the heels of the eleventh-hour cancellation of her Valentine's Day wedding to Trent Jeffreys, founder of Hearts, Hearths & Homes, a nonprofit housing organization.

Whatever the reason, we predict Miss Starr is taking only a brief sabbatical. Producer Max Shapiro agrees, "Faith's tired. She's had a string of bad roles, but she's also at the pinnacle of her career. The right script will have her back in front of the cameras before you know it."

Let's hope so, because all America is waiting.

Chapter One

She was a grand lady built to last. The most beautiful in Berry Patch, Oregon, and she was supposed to be his.

Sitting in his pickup truck, Gabriel Logan stared at the 1908 Craftsman-style mansion—the stone-covered pillars, the multi-paned windows, the exposed beams, the wraparound porch and the three dormers jutting from the long-sloping, gabled roof. She was beautiful, all right. As his heart filled with regret, he tightened his grip on the steering wheel.

For years, he'd been dreaming, planning and saving for the day he would buy this house. Eighty-one-year-old Miss Larabee had promised it to him until two months ago when she'd received another offer "too good to pass up." One she didn't even give him the opportunity to match.

He drummed his fingers against the leather-covered

steering wheel. His dog, Frank, raised his head from the passenger's seat and groaned.

"Sorry, boy." Gabe scratched behind the giant mastiff's drooping ears. "It shouldn't matter. We're here, right? On time. Might as well get to work."

But Gabe made no move to get out of the truck.

Today he started work on his dream house. Not as the owner. As the contractor hired to turn it into a B and B. His grandfather must be rolling in his grave. This house was meant for a family—not tourists with a buzz after visiting one of Willamette Valley's award-winning wineries. Yet Gabe was about to do the dirty work for the mysterious F. S. Addison. He hadn't spoken with the new owner yet. A mutual friend, Henry Davenport, had made all the arrangements. He'd referred more business than Gabe and his crew could handle, and money continued pouring in.

Talk about ironic.

Bitterness coated his mouth. This was one job he didn't want. But Gabe didn't trust anyone else to remodel the house while preserving the character, the charm and the million other things that made it special. Things that made the house a home. What should have been his home.

The title company might not agree, but Gabe and his family had been calling it his house for years.

Frank tried to roll over and expose his belly for rubs, but there wasn't enough room in the king cab.

"Sorry, boy." Gabe patted the dog. "We both got screwed this time around. And not in a good way."

Frank moaned.

"I know the truck is cramped."

With sad eyes, the dog stared up at him. No doubt Frank missed his custom-built doghouse and the large, fenced yard where he'd had room to roam. Gabe missed them, too.

"But I can't leave you at Mom and Dad's during the day. As soon as I have time, I'll find us another house."

When Miss Larabee had told him she was moving to an assisted-living facility, he'd had no doubt her house would be his. So he'd made an offer, put his home up for sale, sold it the next day and moved into the studio above his parents' garage to wait until he could move into Miss Larabee's house. A good plan. If it had worked out.

Too bad none of his plans had worked out so far. Gabe had once thought he had it all figured out. At eighteen, he'd marry his high-school sweetheart, by the time he was thirty, he'd have a minivan full of kids and be living in the Larabee house. Instead he was thirty-two with no wife, no kids and no place to call home.

He stared at the house.

Sorry, Gramps.

His grandfather had wanted to restore the house, too. Death had robbed him of his dream. And now F. S. Addison had robbed Gabe of his.

Frank pawed at the passenger door.

Reaching over two hundred pounds of tan fur, Gabe opened it. The dog poured himself out, lumbered up the walkway and front steps and plopped down on the shady porch. Even Frank acted as if the house was theirs.

Gabe slapped the steering wheel. This wasn't going to be easy, but he couldn't sit in the truck all day.

Time to get moving. The sooner this job was over, the sooner he could get on with his life. He slid out of the truck and sorted through the bucket of blueprints stored in the back of the cab.

Frank barked. Once, twice. A cat? A bloodcurdling-slasher-movie scream cut through the stillness of the summer morning. No, the scream was female, not feline. Gabe sprinted around the front of the truck.

"Frank."

The dog wasn't on the porch.

Another bark.

His deep woofs signaled his location like a beacon. Gabe ran toward the sound, around the front of the house to the side yard. He waded through weeds and too-tall grass to find Frank, with his tail wagging, straddling the trunk of an old maple tree. This was where Gabe had pictured his own kids climbing into a canopy of shade and picnicking beneath its dense branches.

"What kind of trouble did you get us into this time?" Gabe asked.

Frank looked up at the tree and panted.

Gabe peered up to see a jeans-clad bottom. A very feminine, round bottom. A white T-shirt was tucked into the waistband. A brown ponytail hung out the back of a navy baseball cap. Frank had chased lots of animals up trees, but this was a first.

"That's some hunting, boy," Gabe murmured. He didn't know whether to punish or praise the hound. "Go."

The dog moved ten feet away and lay on the grass. Frank kept his head low—his guilty look—and drool ran from the corners of his mouth and pooled on the ground.

A muffled sob floated down from above.

"Are you okay, miss?"

"Is it gone?" a shaky voice asked.

"It?"

"The monster attack d-dog with big teeth. I just wanted to see the front of the house and was walking by…" Her voice was unsure, quiet. Scared.

With five sisters, he knew the sound well. From bugs to snakes to killer clowns, he'd dealt with it all. "You must not be from around here."

"How did you guess?"

First, he would have remembered that bottom. Second, most people in Berry Patch walked in the early evening after they were done with work and had time to chat with neighbors on the street. And third, she was up a tree. "Everyone in town knows Frank's bark is worse than his bite."

"Is Frank short for Frankenstein?"

Gabe grinned. "Frank Lloyd Wright."

Her mouth tightened. She looked down and nearly lost her sunglasses. "Is he still here?"

"The architect is dead, but the dog is right here."

"Real funny." Her voice trembled.

She was really scared. That bothered Gabe. Worried him, too. "Did Frank hurt you?"

"He attacked me."

That made zero sense. Gabe's nieces did everything to Frank and the dog never cared. He sopped up love like a dry sponge. He didn't even mind the baby bibs and bonnets they put on him. "Frank *attacked* you?"

"Well…not exactly," she said. "He barked and ran

toward me. I didn't wait to see what he would do next. I saw this tree and ran."

"Frank's got a bad hip so he lumbers more than runs. Though if he gets excited he can sprint for a short distance," Gabe said. "He must have wanted some attention."

"Or breakfast."

Gabe wouldn't mind a taste himself. Another place, another time… "Come on down out of that tree. Frank might look intimidating, but he's as harmless as a pup."

"Cujo, or your average menacing canine that runs in a pack?"

Scared or not, she was showing some spunk. Gabe grinned. "Newborn puppy. Nearly blind."

She scooted down, bringing her bare ankle and generic white canvas slip-on shoes to his eye level.

"It's okay," he encouraged. "Frank only wanted to play with you."

"I…I don't play with dogs."

"I won't hold it against you."

Gabe hadn't gotten a good look at her face, but she intrigued him. Berry Patch didn't get many visitors, especially young females who could scale trees the way she had. He wondered why she was in town, where she was staying and for how long. Mr. and Mrs. Ritchey, the next-door neighbors, had a daughter who attended a swanky college on the East Coast. Was this one of Brianna Ritchey's friends? He hoped not. Though Gabe didn't like his women that young, if this were Brianna's friend, he would take both girls out to make amends.

"How about I take you out to dinner tonight to make up for Frank chasing you?" Gabe asked.

"Thanks, but that's not necessary."

"Another night?"

No answer. Shot down. Ouch. He'd dated most of the available women in town and still hadn't found what he was looking for. Guess he'd have to keep looking.

She tried to find her footing. Not an easy thing to do in those shoes.

"I'm sorry Frank scared you," Gabe said. "He really is a good dog."

"I don't like dogs," she mumbled.

A huge strike against her, but he really liked the way her jeans fit. And based on that ponytail, her hair had to be long. He liked long hair. "Why not?"

She scooted farther down the tree. "I got bit when I was little."

His sisters had trained him well. He knew the necessary response. "That must have been scary. Was it a big dog or one of those ankle-biting, yipping rat dogs?"

"A rat dog."

The sound of her voice made him think she was smiling. Good. He didn't want her to be afraid. "Those little dogs will get you every time. They're so small they have to assert their dominance."

"Kind of like men driving cars and trucks with more horsepower than they'll ever need."

"Exactly." He grinned. "Though some men do need that extra horsepower. Egos are pretty heavy to haul around."

"Not many men would admit that."

"I'm not 'many men.'"

She glanced down at him, but her sunglasses hid her eyes. "What do you drive?"

He rocked back on his heels. "A pickup with heavy-duty hauling capacity."

He caught a glimmer of a smile.

She climbed down a few more inches. He could see the back of her T-shirt, the band and straps of her bra showing through the stretchy white fabric.

"Would you like help?" he asked.

"I can do it myself."

He knew better than to interfere with a woman on a mission. His mother had taught him that one. "I'm sure you can."

Just then, she lost her footing and slid. He placed his hands on her hips to keep her from falling. She was soft and curvy in all the right places. Her scent, sunshine and grapefruit, surrounded him. Now this was the way to start a morning. Maybe today wouldn't be so terrible after all. He would have to reward Frank with a bone later. Gabe smiled as he lowered her from the tree.

She stood in front of him and brushed her palms against her thighs. "Thank you."

Gabe believed females were gifts from above. They deserved to be cherished and adored. He loved women, but he could really love the one standing in front of him. "At your service, milady."

Most of the women he knew liked a little chivalry, but her full lips didn't break into a smile as he expected. She did raise her chin, giving him a better view of her face. If only she'd remove those sunglasses so he could see her eyes. She wore no makeup, not even lipstick, but she didn't need any. She was lovely. A natural beauty. With a straight, thin nose, generous lips and high cheekbones any model would die for. Her only flaw was a smudge of dirt on her right cheek and that just made her cuter. Though cute and the way the T-shirt stretched over her breasts didn't belong in the same sentence. His temperature shot up.

Something about her rang a bell. Several actually. "Have we met before?"

"No," she said. "I only arrived yesterday afternoon."

Not even nine o'clock on her first morning in town and he'd already met her. Not bad timing. In fact, perfect timing. He definitely owed Frank a treat.

Gabe tried to place where he knew her. "You look familiar."

She pressed her lips together. "I must have one of those faces."

"You're too beautiful to be just a face in the crowd."

She shrugged.

Her indifference didn't sway him. "I know you from somewhere. It's going to come to me."

A squirrel scampered through the overgrown yard. Frank barked, stood on all fours and trotted toward them.

The woman gasped and grabbed hold of Gabe. Her sunglasses flew off. Her hat fell back and long, wavy brown hair cascaded down. She buried her face against him.

He pulled her close. He liked the way she felt in his arms, probably more than he should, but he didn't like the way she trembled; it was worse than one of those Chihuahuas Frank could use as a squeak toy.

"Sit."

Frank obeyed. The action made the time and money of puppy kindergarten and dog-obedience training worth it.

"On the porch. Now."

The dog loped his way to the front of the house.

Gabe continued to hold the woman, waiting for the rapid beating of her heart to slow. Finally it did. "You okay?"

She didn't say a word, but clung to him. It was nice. Though he wished it were under different circumstances. Say, mouth-watering attraction rather than overwhelming fear.

"It's okay if you aren't," he said. "I kind of like standing here with you in my arms. Doesn't happen to a guy like me every day. Now every other day…"

She laughed. He liked the sound.

"What's your name?" he asked.

A slight hesitation. "Faith."

"Pretty name," he said. "I'm Gabe. And we have a problem, Faith."

She tightened her grip. "Frank?"

"He can be a problem, but no, we have another one. You can't see from where you're standing, but Mrs. Henry is peeking out of her miniblinds from across the street and she's got her phone in her hand. She's real tight with Mrs. Bishko and Mrs. Lloyd. The three of them like to keep the fine citizens of Berry Patch informed of all the happenings in town. I don't need that and I doubt you do, either."

"Oh, no. That would be bad." She backed out of his arms. "Thank you."

"You're welcome."

The first thing he noticed was her hair. The color wasn't simply brown, but oiled teak with copper highlights glimmering in the morning sun. Long strands hung over her face, and she flipped those behind her shoulders with a simple motion of her head.

Gabe drew in a quick, sharp breath.

They had never met, but he knew her. Knew all about her. Why hadn't he recognized her immediately? She was, in a word, unforgettable.

The full, kissable lips that curved into an easy smile at the drop of a pin and melted even the coldest heart. The soulful, expressive green eyes that saw everything and made a man question his worth. The wavy mane of chestnut hair meant for covering a pillow or a man's chest. Oh, yeah, he knew exactly who she was. Just like every other person who went to the movies or breathed.

"You're the actress," he said. "Faith Starr."

She looked away. "That's my stage name."

Exactly. Faith was a movie star. One of the most beautiful people in the world. Famous, rich, important. Someone who did not belong here, and he'd asked her out to dinner. Still it would make a good story. Not many men in Berry Patch got the chance to be shot down by a famous actress. "Are they filming a movie around here?"

Faith's mouth drew tight. She put her baseball cap and sunglasses back on. "No."

Funny, but now that he knew who she was, Faith looked more like a famous person with those things on than off.

"What brings you to Berry Patch?" Gabe asked.

"A friend lives here."

He knew everyone in town. "Who is that?"

"Henry Davenport."

"He's a friend of mine, too," Gabe said.

She furrowed her brows. "You're a friend of Henry's?"

"I know his wife." Gabe knew what she was thinking. How could a contractor be the friend of a billionaire? "She's my sister Theresa's best friend."

The edges of Faith's mouth curved upward in a slight smile. Her tension seemed to ease. "Henry Davenport married. I still can't believe it. Husband. Father. Farmer. The Henry I knew wasn't interested in anything but having a good time."

"Nothing wrong with having a good time." That's what Gabe had. One good time after another, but it wasn't what he wanted. Not really. A part of him envied Henry. Not for all his money, but for what he'd found on the Wheeler Berry Farm. Years ago Gabe had thought he'd found the same thing—the woman of his dreams who wanted to raise a family in Berry Patch and live happily ever after. He'd been wrong. "But Henry and Elisabeth are perfect together."

"That's what Henry told me." Faith's smile widened. The effect—dazzling. "I'm so happy for him. I can't wait to meet his wife."

Faith's happiness seemed genuine. Maybe there was more to her than her movie-goddess image. More than her reputation as a runaway bride and heartbreaker. As she stared at the wraparound porch where Frank lay, she narrowed her lips. Then again, maybe not.

"Are you staying a few days?" Gabe asked.

"Actually I plan to stay much longer."

Yeah, right. Someone like Faith would never last more than a couple weeks in this small, quiet town. A month at the most. She would get bored, long for the excitement of a big city and leave. The ambitious ones, women like his ex-wife, always did.

"I'm going to like it here," Faith added. "It's a cute place."

"You haven't been here when it rains. Cute wears off real fast." Though a few nights at the cheesy hotel near Highway 99 or one of the homey, not-so-elegant B and Bs nearby would probably have the same effect. "Where are you staying?"

"Here."

"Here?"

She smiled. "I bought this house."

No.

"Is your last name Addison?" he croaked out the words. "F. S. Addison?"

"I'm Faith Starr Addison. Starr is my middle name and my mother's name." She drew her brows together. "How did you know?"

He ignored the question. "You bought this house from Miss Larabee?"

Faith nodded. "She's so sweet. She reminds me of my late grandmother. We met for the first time last night at dinner. We watched one of my movies together."

"Dinner and a movie?"

"Yes." Faith adjusted her baseball cap. "She asked me for my autograph. She was so cute."

Gabe fought a wave of nausea. He remembered Miss Larabee's one great passion—the movies. She'd once dreamed of being an actress. Damn. Dinner with a movie star must have been the offer "too good to pass up."

Still that didn't explain her selling the house to Faith. Not after he'd shared his own dreams about the house with Miss Larabee over tea during his weekly visits— dreams of restoring the house the way his grandfather had always wanted to do and raising a family here. Guess that couldn't compare to dinner with flighty and flaky Faith, as the press called her, who merely had to learn to smile and speak on cue and steal people's dreams.

She sighed with apparent satisfaction. "Henry was right when he told me it would be perfect for a B and B."

Gabe froze. He couldn't breathe, let alone speak. But he had to. He had to know. "You asked Henry to find you a B and B here in town?"

"No, I'd never heard of Berry Patch," she said. "I hadn't spoken with Henry in months, but he called out of the blue to say hi. We were catching up when I told him about looking for a B and B to buy and he explained how Berry Patch is an up-and-coming tourist destination in the heart of wine country."

Movie star turned innkeeper? That made no sense. "Why would you want a B and B?"

She stiffened. "I always thought I'd go into the hotel business someday."

"I can't see you as innkeeper."

She raised her chin. "I spent a lot of time working at inns and B and Bs when I was a teenager." A slight smile formed on her lips. "You should taste my stuffed French toast."

An invitation? He didn't think so. Besides Gabe wasn't interested. She was the enemy. Hell, she was his worst nightmare. The kind of woman his ex-wife had wanted to be. And now he worked for her on a house that should belong to him.

"After Henry told me about this house, he e-mailed me pictures. I made an offer that day. Everything went so smoothly I have to believe it was fate."

Not fate. Henry. Damn him.

Gabe felt as if he'd been hit in the gut. And it was his friend, Henry, throwing the punches. A mix of emotions swirled inside Gabe. Anger, frustration, betrayal. He clenched his fists.

It was all Henry's fault.

No, it wasn't. Henry didn't know about Gabe's dream of owning this house. It wasn't something they discussed over beers at The Vine. He had only shared the plan of his life with his family and Miss Larabee.

"Is something wrong?" Faith asked.

Very wrong. And now he knew why.

The owner's notes—containing glitzy, glamorous and thoroughly modern changes to the remodeling plans—he'd received via Henry suddenly made a lot more sense. Gabe didn't like the notes or her.

"You aren't what I expected," he said finally.

"I never am," she murmured with a faraway look in her eyes. But in a moment, her gaze sharpened. "So I have a couple of questions for you. Who are you? And why is your dog sleeping on my front porch?"

My front porch.

Gabe bristled at the words. Resentment overflowed. There was so much he wanted to say to her. "I quit" was tops on the list. He glanced at the house.

Remember what's important.

It wasn't Faith. Or him.

It was this house.

His grandfather had been obsessed with restoring it for as long as Gabe could remember. It hadn't taken long for him to feel the same way. Each time the bus passed by here on his way to school, his own desire had intensified. But when he'd accompanied his grandfather to fix a leak for Miss Larabee, something had happened. Something that went deeper than the house.

Even though Gabe had only been fourteen at the time, everything he wanted in life had crystallized during that first visit—a wife, kids, a dog and this house. The perfect family living the perfect life in the perfect house.

A life totally different from his own.

His family had been far from perfect. Too many kids, too many animals and a house that was nothing more than fodder for a wrecking ball.

He wanted that perfect life. Desperately.

Gabe had made a plan and set out to achieve it. He'd married the girl of his dreams right after high-school graduation. Next on the list were children. But his wife hadn't wanted to stay in Berry Patch. He hadn't wanted to leave. So they'd divorced.

But he wasn't about to let his dream die. Unlike his father, when Gabe made a plan he stuck to it. So what if his first wife hadn't gone along with his blueprint for a perfect life? So what if Henry had messed up Gabe's chance of buying this house? So what if Miss Larabee had sold the house out from under him?

Gabe wasn't giving up.

He had to remain strong, steadfast, to protect the house from Faith.

Already the second floor suffered from remuddling—what happened when remodeling destroyed the character of a home—and he wasn't about to allow any more damage to be done. And that's what would happen if he followed through with the changes suggested by F. S. Addison. But Gabe wasn't about to do that. He would succeed with the Larabee house where his grandfather had failed with the farmhouse Gabe grew up in. The mess of a house his parents still called home.

While Gabe was growing up, his father had ignored Grandpa's suggestions about remodeling the house. Instead of having a plan, his father took whatever extra money he had and simply added on whatever space he thought they needed most. But the money never lasted due to a tractor needing a new engine or some other farming mishap, so his dad just stopped whatever he was building. He never finished anything. Gabe's bedroom had been nothing more than drywall and Astroturf for more years than he cared to remember. He'd had to finish it himself when he got older. And his sister Cecilia's room, too. If not for him, the house would still be a bunch of unfinished rooms and additions.

"Are you going to answer my questions?" She sounded annoyed he'd ignored her for so long.

It was just the sort of snotty pay-attention-to-me-now attitude he expected from the actress, but she was the client. And until she got tired of the country and this house, he was stuck with her.

"Frank is asleep on the porch because he goes wherever I go." With Gabe's emotions firmly tucked back in place, his tone was cool but professional. "I'm Gabriel Logan. The contractor you hired to re-model the house."

Chapter Two

Oh, my. Oh, no.

Forget about the killer canine with the massive jaws and thundering bark. The man was the bigger threat. To her peace of mind. To her plans. To her future.

Faith lowered the brim of her baseball cap, thankful the sunglasses shielded the surprise in her eyes. "You're Gabriel Logan?"

He didn't say anything. Just gave a single nod.

She had expected a balding middle-aged contractor, not sex in a tool belt.

Curly brown hair fell past his collar. Long khaki shorts and a green T-shirt showed off his lean-but-strong body. A far cry from an Armani suit, but the casual style fit him. Nicely.

Tall, dark and...

Ruggedly handsome was the only way to describe

him. He could easily give Hollywood's latest "it" boy a run for his money. Long, dark lashes fringed sapphire eyes. Fine lines at the corners of his eyes softened the chiseled planes of his face, a strong jaw and a nose that looked as if it had been broken at least once.

Her heart pounded, and her stomach tingled.

Uh-oh. It always started like this. The shiver of awareness. The air of anticipation.

She was in trouble. A whole lot of trouble.

The last thing she wanted was a man in her life. She wasn't looking to fall in love. She'd fallen more times than she could count, but she hadn't found "the one."

Her one true love.

The way every other Addison had before her. No one had divorced or even separated during the past two hundred years of her family's recorded history. Faith wasn't about to ruin the streak. She'd failed enough.

Broken engagements. Broken hearts. Broken promises.

She wasn't giving an encore performance.

That's why she'd sunk every penny she had into this B and B project. Renovating an old house had to be easier than finding her one true love. She might not join the ranks of her family who had found their soul mates, but she could certainly join them in their successful hotel business, Starr Properties and Resorts.

A much saner business than acting.

Faith would prove to her mother—to her entire family—that despite making some huge mistakes in the past, she didn't need a man to take care of her. She could do it herself.

"Henry's told me a lot about you," Faith said. But

not enough. Not nearly enough. She'd wanted a contractor who was competent, experienced and safe. Two out of three…

"He told me nothing about you," Gabriel said.

"I asked him not to."

He narrowed his eyes. "Why?"

"I didn't want you to accept the job because of who I am."

"Not likely."

At least he wasn't starstruck. Men often treated her differently because of who she was, or rather who they thought she was. Their reactions disappointed more than hurt. She tucked a strand of hair back into her cap. "I also didn't want my involvement leaked to the press."

She needed this project to remain a secret. She wanted to fix up the house, sell the renovated B and B to Starr Properties without her family knowing it was hers and show her family she was not only ready but capable of taking her rightful place in the business. She was as much an Addison as they were, even if she had never made it to "I do" and had made a mess of pretty much everything in her life.

Gabriel stared at her in disbelief. "You thought I'd call the *Berry Patch Gazette* and brag that I was working for some movie star?"

Gabriel sounded affronted. Disgusted, too. But it had happened to Faith before. A tabloid had paid one of her ex-fiancés for an exposé of their relationship. "It's not the *Berry Patch Gazette* I'm worried about. Tabloids pay a lot and I don't want the publicity."

"I thought there was no such thing as bad publicity."

"Try remodeling a house with sixty photographers taking pictures of you all day."

"I wouldn't want to."

"Then it's a good thing no one knows about this house." Faith forced a when-is-this-press-junket-going-to-end smile. "Or me."

Gabriel's jaw tensed and she wondered what had caused the sudden change in him. A few minutes earlier he'd been flirting and asking her out on a date. Now he looked as tense as her stomach felt. She didn't want him to quit. According to Henry, he was the best and she needed all the help she could get. She couldn't afford another mistake. Not now. Not with this.

Time to make nice. She removed her sunglasses, stuck them above the brim of her cap and wiped her sweaty palms on her jeans. "It's good to finally meet you."

He didn't say anything.

Faith extended her arm. A second passed. And another. Finally his large hand engulfed hers. His skin was rough, his grip firm. Strong. He drew his hand back and she was relieved not to be touching him. He was too warm, too male. Too much.

She waited for him to say something. Anything. A false nicety. An insincere compliment or two.

Nothing.

A flicker of apprehension coursed through her.

Faith fought against it. Gabriel had picked the wrong woman if he thought she was going to give up so easily. "So you're a licensed contractor?"

Another nod.

"And you own your own business?"

"Yes."

This was worse than trying to get an extra ticket on Oscar night. Maybe he was sulking because she'd shot him down.

Luckily she hadn't accepted his dinner offer. She'd been tempted. That whole knight-fantasy thing when she'd been in the tree had been very appealing. Knights were heroic. Knights were romantic. Knights took charge. But for once that wasn't what she needed. Or wanted. Thank goodness she'd listened to her head, not her heart, and avoided making a huge mistake.

She would continue to do the same where Gabriel Logan was concerned.

"How many employees do you have?" she asked.

"Four."

If only she could get four words out of him. "Thanks for sending me the remodeling plans. Did Henry give you the questionnaire with my comments?"

Yet another nod. "Did you receive the revised plans?"

Six words. Maybe Gabriel hadn't failed Customer Service 101 and they were starting to get somewhere. "Yes, I did. Thank you. I like what you did with the kitchen."

Her compliment didn't draw the reaction she'd expected. If anything he looked annoyed. "Do you have any questions or…changes?" The words seemed to stick in his throat.

Definitely annoyed. "Yes. A few things." Several, actually. "My notes are in the carriage house."

Gabriel furrowed his brow. "The carriage house?"

"That's where I'm staying." After buying this house, she couldn't afford a motel, let alone a hotel or

B and B. "I want to be close to the house while the re-modeling is going on."

"It's going to be noisy. Dirty."

"A little dust never bothered me."

"A construction site isn't a movie set."

"I've been on sets in the jungle, the mountains and the desert," she countered. "It's not all five-star hotels with Evian baths if that's what you're thinking. I can handle a lot more than dust."

He didn't say anything. Again. He'd been so warm to her earlier, but now he was so cold she needed a sweater. She didn't get it. Or him.

"I have the plans in the truck." Gabriel walked away before she could reply. Faith followed him to the front yard, but kept a good distance from the porch with its slumbering mascot. She had more to be concerned about than the dog. She stared at Gabriel.

He strutted up the stone walkway with a confident stride. Staring at him, her mouth went dry. She forced herself to look away.

What was going on?

Her reactions to him made no sense. She'd been surrounded by gorgeous men her entire life. Thanks to Rio Rivers and her string of costars and fiancés, she'd become immune to them. So why was Gabriel Logan having such an affect on her? She blew out a puff of air.

"Today I was planning to do a walk-through, verify the drawings and check dimensions." He glanced at his watch. "My crew will be here later to remove fixtures and cap off electrical sockets, but I thought I'd go in now."

"I'd love to help." She sounded more confident than she felt. As always. No problem. Surely she could play the role of knowledgeable, self-reliant B and B owner? "If it's no problem?"

His gaze raked over her. If the hard glint in his eyes was anything to go by, her presence was a problem. Faith wasn't about to be deterred.

"Before I forget, I have something for you." She reached into her pocket and pulled out two keys. As she handed one to Gabriel, her fingers brushed his warm skin and tingles raced up her arm. Faith jerked her hand away. "You're going to need this."

As he stared at the key in his palm, his frown deepened.

"Don't you need a key?" she asked.

"Yes."

Another monosyllabic response. Not even a thank-you.

What was his problem? She fought the urge to chew on the inside of her cheek. "Is something wrong?"

The blue of his eyes deepened. "No."

She didn't believe him. He looked dark and danger-ous. Like a bad boy. A really bad boy. Make that a black knight. An unexpected rush of heat whipped through her.

Suddenly Henry Davenport's assurances meant very little. They weren't going to make Gabriel Logan the right man for the job. Or, a little voice whispered, the right man for her.

Standing on the porch, Gabe tightened his fingers around the house key. This wasn't the way he'd planned to get it.

He knew where Miss Larabee kept a spare hidden

on the back porch. That's how his crew had gotten inside to take the measurements for the floor plan.

Now, to be given his own key...but he couldn't forget, it was only temporarily his.

Gabe shoved it into his pocket. With a heavy heart, he watched Faith insert her key into the lock of the double oak doors.

Her hand trembled. "I'm dying to see the inside."

"Haven't you seen the place before?"

"No," she admitted. "I was tempted to peek last night, but it was too late by the time I returned from dinner."

Great, now he wasn't only her contractor but also her tour guide.

The lock clicked open. She smiled. "Here goes nothing."

Eagerness filled her voice, but the only thing he felt was dread pressing down on him like a two-ton weight. He wanted her to hate the house. He wanted her to regret her decision. He wanted her gone.

But he knew it wasn't going to happen. Anyone with half a brain would love the house the minute she stepped inside.

As the door opened, the old hinges didn't squeak. They didn't make a sound. Pride filled him. All these years, he'd taken care of the house's routine maintenance—or at least the minor things Miss Larabee had allowed him to do for her.

He'd been waiting for the day when he could fix everything. That day had finally arrived. But what should have been a dream come true was a living nightmare.

Gabe wrapped his fingers around the remodeling plans until the paper crinkled. He loosened his grip.

Faith glanced at him. "I guess I'm a little nervous."

Nervous didn't begin to describe how he felt. Gabe had imagined this moment for years. Carrying his bride over the threshold the first time they entered the house, their house.

But Faith Starr wasn't his wife, and the house wasn't his.

"It won't bite," he said.

Her lips curved into a slight smile. "Frank? Or the house?"

"Neither."

She walked inside. Unfortunately the house didn't swallow her up and spit her outside.

Which meant it was his turn.

"Are you coming?" Faith asked.

A beat passed. He drew a deep breath and stepped over the threshold into the foyer.

Faith was already oohing and aahing the way he knew she would. He couldn't wait to see her reaction when she saw the rest of the house, especially the upstairs.

"All these windows and French doors. It's so bright and open." Faith's mouth formed a perfect O, and she glanced around. She reminded him of his nieces when he took them to the toy store. "And spacious. I had no idea it would be so big."

"It's a lot of square footage." But Faith's presence filled the room, the house. The large, empty space was more welcoming with her here. Star quality? It couldn't be anything else.

"The hardwood floors are lighter than I thought they would be."

"They need to be refinished." Gabe wanted to find as much fault as possible so she would get discouraged and give it up. "With the room empty, you can see how dingy and scratched the floors are."

"They're still nice." She knelt to touch the hardwood, giving him a great view of her bottom. Courtesy of a highly paid personal trainer, no doubt. "And they give the house a warm, homey feel."

A black mouse scurried across the floor. Cobwebs and dust bunnies weren't the only things to have taken up residence since Miss Larabee had moved out.

"We're going to need a cat," Faith said.

He'd expected her to scream. Or at least gasp.

She'd done neither.

So, tiny furry things didn't scare her, only big ones that barked. He'd have to remember that.

"There could be other things lurking beneath the baseboards," he warned.

"I'll call an exterminator." She smiled. "Or Frank."

The edges of Gabe's mouth curved. He couldn't help himself. Her charm drew him in even though that was the last thing he wanted. He would have to watch it. Watch her. She'd already stolen his house. He couldn't give her a shot at his heart.

Faith stepped into the sitting area on the left. "The fireplace, the exposed beams on the ceiling. It's absolutely perfect."

He forced his gaze off her and into the room. At least she had the right enthusiasm about the house. That had to count for something. Maybe he'd misjudged her. It wouldn't be the first time he'd done that.

As much as he liked women he didn't always have the best judgment of their nature or motives. He'd seen only what he'd wanted to see in his ex-wife. He wouldn't make that mistake again.

"Oh, look. Another seating area—" she hurried back across the entry into the room on the right-hand side of the house "—with another fireplace. This is great. Guests can have their choice of areas to sit and relax."

Guests. Not a family.

Her enthusiasm wasn't so appealing after all.

She stood in front of a window, the spot where he had imagined putting up a Christmas tree, and pointed to a corner. "What a perfect place for a Christmas tree."

"Where you're standing is better."

Damn. He hadn't meant to say that.

She glanced around. "You're right."

He didn't want to be right. Not about the tree, the house or its new owner.

As Faith walked across the room, the air moved around her. She exuded an energy he could almost touch. It made zero sense but he wanted to touch it.

Touch her.

Gabe brushed a cobweb from the ceiling.

"I can't believe the staircase. The wood is incredible." Her gaze met his. "Can you match the trim and moldings if they need to be replaced? Arts and Crafts style is popular, but these designs are so old."

He liked that she cared about the details. Liked it a lot. Stop. Focus on business, the house. Anything but her. "The finishing work can be specially milled to match."

"But won't you be able to tell what's new versus old?"

"When my crew and I are finished, you won't know the difference." He ran his hand down one of the wide staircase's balustrades. The polished wood felt smooth and solid. This house had stood long before he and Faith were born and would be around long after they were gone. "My goal when I remodel an old house is to have the place look as if I've never been there and have all the work I've done look as if it's been there forever."

"That's a noble goal," she said. "But is it realistic with all the modern conveniences people expect nowadays? And staying within budget?"

As if money were a concern to a famous movie star...

"Yes to both questions," Gabe answered anyway. Maybe she would get tired of the house and Berry Patch the way she got tired of her fiancés. "Many people long for the charm and character of an older home, but don't want to sacrifice a gourmet kitchen or a spa-like bath or closet space. With care and planning, restoration can be achieved without ruining the architectural integrity of the house or costing an arm and a leg."

Her eyes twinkled. "Good answers."

He didn't care what she thought. "It's my job."

"The Ornaments of a House Are the Friends that Frequent It." She touched the inscription over the fireplace. The faded gold letters were raised on an oak plank and inset in the bricks. "Isn't that just perfect for a B and B?"

Better for a family home. "No."

"What did you say?" she asked.

Busted. Like it or not, she was the client. If he provoked her enough, Faith could fire him and hire someone else. Someone like Scott Ellis and his crew of imbeciles who would do whatever she wanted as long as she was willing to pay for it. Gabe couldn't allow that to happen.

Time for damage control. "The quote is from Emerson."

She arched a brow. "You don't seem like the poetry type."

"I'm just a guy from a small town who pounds nails for a living. I'm not much into types."

"What are you into?" she asked.

The interest in her voice kicked up his desire, aroused him. He clamped it down. Not now. And not with her.

"Poetry?" she suggested.

"Sometimes." He hooked his thumb through a belt loop. "I'm into houses, architecture, family and friends. My dog."

You. Like her or not, she was attractive. Sexy. A whole lot of other things that he didn't want to think about.

"What about you?" Gabe stared at her. He shouldn't be interested in her, but the question had slipped out. "What are you into?"

"My family. Especially my nieces and nephew. And my privacy."

If that was supposed to be a hint, he wasn't taking it. Berry Patch wasn't her home. She had no family here. Sure she might have some privacy, but not as an innkeeper. Maybe she wasn't that committed to this project. To this house. Maybe his dream wasn't completely dead. "How do those things fit into owning a B and B?"

"They're why I'm here." She tilted her chin. "Why I bought this house. And why I want the best contractor around to remodel it."

He couldn't deny her compliment pleased him, but the determination in her voice surprised him and aroused his curiosity.

Better keep his mind on the house. Gabe didn't usually mind mixing business with pleasure, but not on this job.

She stepped into the dining room and he followed her.

In the sunlight flooding the room, her hair looked almost auburn. Her lips curled into an easy smile. "The built-ins are beautiful."

He forced himself not to stare at her. Stay focused. "The French doors lead to a small back porch."

She peered out. "Cozy."

Too cozy.

Time to put an end to this. He didn't want her to like the house. He wanted her to hate it. And he knew how to make that happen. She needed to see the upstairs. ASAP.

Gabriel motioned to the second staircase around the corner. "That's the maid's staircase. Would you like to see the bedrooms upstairs?"

Chapter Three

Conscious of the big contractor on her heels, Faith hurried up the steep, narrow kitchen staircase. The higher she climbed, the heavier and more stagnant the air felt. If this was a movie, music foreshadowing impending doom would play on the sound track and the audience would inch forward on their seats.

But this wasn't a movie. And her instincts were on high alert. Not that she could trust her instincts. That was just one of the many lessons she'd learned this year.

Another step, and she heard a hissing sound. She froze.

Gabriel bumped into her backside and grabbed her waist so she wouldn't stumble. His hands were big and strong. Heat flooded her cheeks. What was going on? She hadn't blushed in years.

"Is something wrong?" he asked.

Oh, yes. Something was definitely wrong, and it had nothing to do with the house, and everything to do with her contractor. The imprints of Gabriel's palms burned their way through her jeans and onto her skin. Hot. Oh, so hot. It felt good. She felt good. And that was very bad considering what was at stake.

"Faith?" His warm breath caressed the back of her neck and he squeezed her gently. "Are you okay?"

No. Not with him so close. She forced herself to breathe.

"I heard something." She turned toward Gabriel, leaving him no choice but to remove his hands. An odd mixture of regret and relief surged through her. "A snake. But why would it be upstairs? It must have been something else."

The stairwell was too dark to read his expression. "It was difficult for Miss Larabee to climb the stairs so she hasn't been up here in years. The upstairs may come as a shock to you."

"Thanks for the warning, but I'm not easily shocked."

Eager to put some distance between them, Faith continued up the stairs. What she had said was true. Even when she had been lured into an interview on an over-rated entertainment cable show and surprised with the appearance of three of her ex-fiancés, she had managed to keep her cool. Nothing could surprise her more than that.

Or so she had thought.

On the landing, she stared in disbelief and horror. As a snake slithered under a doorway, a *Weekly-Secrets*-tabloid-size lump formed in her throat.

The faded, peeling blue-and-purple hydrangea wall-paper and the dingy, stained carpet made the landing and adjacent hallway dark and claustrophobic. Only random pools of sunlight reminded her that she stood on the second story, not underground. Or in a cave.

A trio of geckos raced across the floor, and doubts swept over her. The house was infested with mice and reptiles. Worse, it was a disaster area up here.

Tears stung her eyes, and she blinked them away.

She only liked to cry on cue.

Any other time was unacceptable.

Faith needed to pull this off, but how?

She was nearly broke. What money she had left was going to the house and remodeling. There was no extra. And that meant she had to rely on Gabriel to stay within the budget. But would he?

Could he?

He didn't like her. She could tell by the disapproval in his eyes. He was one more person in a long line of people who made snap judgments based on who they thought she was. Any other time it wouldn't have mattered. But standing here in her version of *The Money Pit,* it did. Faith straightened, not about to let her desperation show. "It just needs a little more work."

"I can't wait to hear your definition of 'a little work.'"

A hard edge laced his words. Faith ignored it. She wasn't going to let Mr. Toolbelt, or this house, get to her.

Maybe Faith wasn't one-hundred-percent ready to handle this project, but she was determined to stay on time, on budget and get the job done, which is what she would be expected to do once she worked for Starr Properties. She wanted to prove to her family she was finished making the wrong choices—fiancés, finances, career.

"Right now, it feels like a lot of work," she said. "But my mother always told me anything is possible."

Those words had kept Faith going. Through the press frenzy, through the broken engagements, through near bankruptcy and her disintegrating career. But even her optimistic mother believed Faith couldn't take care of herself and needed to marry.

Faith breathed deeply to gather her strength and nearly choked on the stale air. A sign? She hoped not. She wanted to embrace everything about this project. Put her heart and her soul into making it a success. But right now she was seriously tempted to hand over the keys, head to her parents' Lake Tahoe house and admit defeat.

"You would have no trouble selling the house if you wanted to walk away," he said.

"Walk away," she echoed.

She could. No one knew what she was doing here except Henry. And he wouldn't tell. She could give up, accept her limitations and a purely figurehead position at Starr Properties until her mother coaxed Faith into marriage so she'd have someone to take care of her.

Now that would be a total disaster.

She squared her shoulders. "I'm not walking away."

"If you're sure…"

"I am." She said the words more for her benefit than his. "Even if the upstairs is…"

"Horrible," he suggested.

"Yes."

"Dank and dingy?"

"A little."

"Overwhelming?" he asked.

"A lot overwhelming, but that's okay," she admitted. "It will make the transformation all the more stunning."

Gabriel studied her for a long moment. "If it's any consolation, I felt the same way the first time I came up here."

His concession seemed reluctant, but she appreciated it just the same.

He continued. "I'd never been inside a mansion before and was so impressed with the architecture and feel of the downstairs. It felt like..."

"Home?"

"Home," he echoed.

She'd felt the same way. Funny, but Gabriel seemed to take the project—this house—very personally and that appealed to her. She wondered if he always did that. Maybe that explained why he had such a good reputation as a contractor.

"But when we walked upstairs, I thought I'd entered the *Twilight Zone*."

"Exactly." Relief washed over her. It wasn't just her. Still, being at the same place as her hunky contractor wasn't much better. She needed distance from him, not to feel as if they were on the same team.

"But I saw the potential," Gabriel added.

And she did, too. Lots of potential. As she stared at him, butterflies flitted about her stomach. Too much potential.

"Good bones," he said.

She gulped. "Excuse me?"

"The house has good bones," he repeated. "Potential."

"Right. Potential." Faith had forgotten he was talking about the house. Maybe if she focused on the house instead of Gabriel, she would see what he'd seen.

She studied the doorways, imagined walls gone and focused on the so-called bones of the structure. Faith widened her eyes. She squinted.

"What are you doing?" Gabriel asked.

"Trying to see the potential."

"And?"

Faith liked looking at him better. "I'm not quite there yet."

She wasn't even close.

The corners of his mouth lifted. Not exactly as flirtatious a smile as before, but the ogre who'd made an earlier appearance seemed to have gone into hiding. "You might not see it, but it's there. Beneath the ugly interior and horrible remodeling and all the snakes and lizards."

When he spoke, his voice had an almost reverent tone, and his eyes softened. Faith felt a tugging on her heart. One day she hoped a man would look at her like that. Not with adoration and envy as other men had, but with respect and appreciation. For her bones, for her soul, for her.

Warmth spread. Suddenly it wasn't about the house. Not at all. She looked away. "Why doesn't the upstairs match the style of the downstairs?"

Something—relief?—flashed in his eyes.

"Miss Larabee's uncle remodeled the second floor

after he inherited the house from her grandparents," Gabriel explained without missing a beat. "He didn't take into account the style of the house. Just moved walls to make extra rooms for his reptile collection."

"That explains the geckos."

"And the snakes. Some of Miss Larabee's relatives were a bit on the eccentric side. According to her, that is." He motioned for Faith to follow him into one of the rooms. "Take a look at the woodwork in this bedroom."

A chameleon sat on a windowsill. She tried not to stare at it and focused on the room instead. All the trim in the large room and framing the two multi-paned windows was painted white. The doors were, too. The color was more dove-gray due to age and dirt, but she knew where he was going with this. Faith smiled. "The white makes the room look brighter."

Gabriel frowned. "White trim in a Craftsman home should be a felony."

Okay. She was wrong. He didn't like white trim. She wondered what else he didn't like. Redheads? Brunettes? Focus on the house. Not on him. "Why?"

"It ruins the integrity of the house."

"What if I like white?" she asked.

"Find another house."

Or another contractor.

The unspoken words hung in the air. She felt them, and from the grim look on Gabriel's face, so did he.

So what happened next?

Gabriel had all the right tools and vocabulary and seemed to love the house. He'd also been the most highly recommended and the least expensive of the three remodeling bids she'd received. She really couldn't afford for him to quit, but he was so possessive, acting as if the house were his, not hers. She'd dealt with this in Hollywood and let others take charge of *her* career. She would not do the same with *her* house. Faith tilted her chin. "I would never do anything to ruin this house."

A muscle throbbed at his jaw. "If you say so."

"I do." She could tell he didn't believe her, and that was okay. For now. She'd prove differently soon enough.

Gabriel Logan was a purist when it came to architectural integrity. Fine. As long as he was willing to do what needed to be done to turn the house into a showcase for Starr Properties.

"Is there a list of other Craftsman-style dos and don'ts you can give me so I avoid 'felony-worthy' suggestions?" she asked.

"No. It's all in here." He pointed to his head. "I remember everything."

"Everything?"

As he nodded, his eyes darkened. "I even remember the time you played a mermaid."

That had been for the film *In Deep Waters*. Gabriel's stark appraisal made her uncomfortable, naked. "I had a body double for the, um, the—"

"Topless shots?"

She crossed her arms in front of her chest. "Yes."

"I was actually remembering the mermaid's determination. You remind me of her feistiness. Not her breasts. Or rather her body double's breasts."

Faith doubted he meant the words as a compliment,

but she'd take them. *Feisty* was better than being a doormat.

"How do you plan to restore the architectural integrity of the original design?" she asked.

An unexpected smile brightened Gabriel's face, and Faith's heart beat a little faster.

"Very carefully," he said.

The gleam in his eyes told Faith her question had impressed him. Finally. She shouldn't care. This was business. Nothing personal. And maybe if she kept telling herself that, the warm glow racing through her veins would go away.

"Miss Larabee gave me the original floor plans years ago, so I know what the architect intended the house to look like."

"Why would she give you the plans?"

He hesitated, as if choosing his words carefully. "I'm a fan of Craftsman architecture and I…I've been wanting to restore the house based on the original plans."

Those were exactly the words she needed to hear. "So we both have a vested interest in making this house the best it can be."

"The best it can be," he repeated.

His tone wasn't filled with much enthusiasm, but it was a start. Faith smiled. "So where do we start?"

"The master bedroom and bath."

"The honeymoon suite?"

A slight wince preceded his nod.

"Lead the way." She followed him into the largest bedroom and ignored the black walls, pea-green ceiling and tarantulas. "This is going to be the premier suite at the B and B, full of romance and elegance. It's where a bride and groom can spend their first night as man and wife. Where a couple can celebrate an anniversary or have a romantic getaway from the kids."

"I figured that out from your notes." He walked past the wood-burning fireplace and into the bathroom. The tiled shower and claw-foot tub gave the space character, but mold and mildew had taken over fighting for turf with a bunch of snakes. Tiles were missing and cracked. The bathroom's saving grace was its size.

But with Gabriel in here, the space seemed smaller. Intimate. Everywhere she turned he seemed to be there. His scent—soap: Irish Spring to be exact—wrapped around her like a hug from an old friend. It washed away all the awful odors and reminded her of…home. Not the stunning contemporary house her parents lived in, but the charming, homey B and B where she'd grown up.

"Can we talk about your ideas for the decor of the master bath?" he asked.

"I want a romantic, fantasy bathroom," she explained. "Marble, double Jacuzzi tub, two-person shower, pedestal sink, gold or brass fixtures."

"Sounds Victorian."

"Yes." Pride filled her. She'd worked hard on the design to make it perfect. No room for mistakes on this project. "The bedroom will match. A brass bed. Lace curtains. Antiques."

Faith waited for Gabriel to tell her what a great job she'd done and dispel her mounting doubts.

His lips thinned. "This house isn't a Victorian."

"It's a Craftsman," she said. "But it's just one room."

His nostrils flared. "Each room is a piece of the whole and needs to be consistent."

"The house *will* be consistent. High quality and craftsmanship. Luxurious furnishings and accessories."

"Consistent. Sure," he said. "I bet Uncle Larabee thought the hallway was just a hallway and no one would care if he boxed up the space. Or put up garish wallpaper. Or—"

"White trim in the bedrooms?" she offered.

"Yes."

"I see your point." But Faith didn't like it. Not after she'd worked so hard. And her ideas were good ones, perfect for a Starr Properties B and B. Still, she and Gabriel would have to work together. She wasn't inflexible and if they came up with something better... "So which part don't you like?"

Gabriel stared at the plans.

Her stomach sank. "You don't like any of my ideas."

He glanced up. "The antique pedestal sink is a nice touch."

"And the rest?"

"It's too...frilly."

"Marble is not frilly."

"True," he said. "It's just plain wrong."

Disappointment pressed down on her. Faith wondered if the awful feeling knotting her insides was what parents felt when overhearing their baby was ugly.

"Craftsman has clean lines, natural materials, warmth," he explained. "Whereas Victorian is ornate, ostentatious, overdone."

"Victorian style is romantic." She gritted her teeth. "I want romance."

"Don't we all."

His heated gaze met hers. Her heart skipped a beat. Three, actually.

Uh-oh. Warning bells rang. Lights flashed. Trouble stood right in front of her and it had another name—Gabriel.

Get a grip, Faith. This was not the time to lose it over her contractor.

She stared at the cracked mirror.

"You've got the two-person Jacuzzi tub, a dual-headed shower and a bed," he said. "What else do you need for romance?"

You. Faith's breath caught in her throat. She didn't need a man to sweep in and make her life complete. She would do that herself.

"You'll have more than enough for 'romance' in here by following the Craftsman tradition," Gabriel continued. "Trust me."

Trust him?

No way.

She wasn't about to trust anyone. That's what had messed up her finances, her career, her heart...

He motioned around the room. "This house could be a showpiece if remodeled correctly."

Aha. She finally got it. His purist views extended to the interior design. Gabriel had his own vision for the house. One he didn't want to give up. She couldn't afford an emotional attachment to the house or its architectural style the way Gabriel seemed to have. She wasn't going to live here, only use the house to achieve her goal. A goal she couldn't allow herself to be sidetracked from.

So, which one of them was right about the master suite? And were they going to be arguing over every single room in the house?

"There are enough Craftsman aficionados that you wouldn't have to rely only on wine-tasting visitors," he added. "The house itself would be the draw."

That appealed to her. To a point.

"I don't want this house to be a living history project. I want it to have a home-away-from-home, old-fashioned air, but have all the modern conveniences guests expect."

"You can still have that."

She did not like his possessive tone. "I *will* have that."

A muscle ticked at his jaw. His dark eyes told her he wasn't pleased. She waited for him to say no. Or quit.

A part of her wanted him to storm out. Another wanted him to stay.

"You hired me for my expertise," he said. "I'm only doing my job."

Faith released the breath she'd been holding. This was so much more than just a house to her, more than a re-modeling project. It was about her family. And her future.

"I'll be the first to admit I don't know everything," she said. "I want your expertise. I need it."

Gabriel shifted his weight. "I'm here to help."

His tone told her those words hadn't been easy for him to say. She appreciated his effort, but she needed more from him than that. "I'm happy to hear that. And you can help me by listening to my input about the house. My house."

His mouth tightened.

She fought the urge to bite the inside of her cheek. "Are you willing to do that? Or should I find another contractor?"

A beat passed. And another.

"I can do that."

Thank goodness. She bit back a sigh. One step closer, but they weren't there yet. "The final decisions have to be mine."

"Fine," he said. "All of the decisions will be yours."

Which meant, she realized with a sinking heart, that all the mistakes would be hers, too.

Following a late lunch at the Wheeler Berry Farm with Henry and Elisabeth Davenport, Faith leaned back in her chair. "So what were you thinking?"

"About what?" Henry asked.

"Recommending Gabriel Logan."

"He's a great contractor and a nice guy." Henry glanced over at her. "Is there a problem?"

"Yes. No. Maybe."

He smiled. "If this is how you approached all your fiancés, it's no wonder you never got to 'I do.'"

"Very funny."

"No, you dating Rio Rivers and having him propose to you live on *Extra!* was funny."

Faith downed the rest of her homemade strawberry lemonade. "Not if you'd been there."

"At least you had the courage to say no."

"I wanted to break his nose."

"You should have. I'm sure he could have had it fixed. Again." Henry poured her another glass of lemonade. "How old was he? Sixteen?"

"Twenty-two."

Henry raised a brow. "And you are?"

"Older than him." She took a deep breath, not wanting to relive her latest romantic misadventure with anyone, including good-natured, charming Henry. "I made the mistake of taking an on-screen romance offscreen."

Again.

But that was the last time. She was through making movies, through being in love with love, through making the wrong choices. Faith toyed with her napkin.

"And now that you've had your boy-toy fun, you're ready to find your perfect match," Henry said.

Perfect match? Such a thing might exist for every one else, but it didn't exist for her.

"That's the last thing I'm ready for," Faith admitted. Five broken engagements. A sixth, had she given in to the pressure of the lights and camera in her face and accepted Rio's ill-timed proposal. Just the idea of spending the rest of her life with any man sent a shiver down her spine. How could she know if she'd found her one true love? How could she know that she wasn't marrying the wrong man?

Henry's hazel eyes darkened. "But you're young, beautiful."

Neither of those meant lucky in love. Faith shrugged.

"Your biological clock is going to start ticking."

"Wait a minute," she said. "You just said I was young."

"You are," he backtracked. "But in a few short years—"

"Don't listen to him, Faith." Elisabeth entered the

room carrying plates of marionberry pie. "I know what he's doing."

Henry's smile softened as he looked at his pregnant wife. "What's that, darling?"

"You're playing matchmaker," Elisabeth said.

"Moi?" Henry acted shocked. "I wouldn't consider such a thing. Maybe once. But not now."

Thank goodness. Faith breathed a sigh of relief. Henry was infamous for his matchmaking, and she wanted no part of it. "So you're not trying to set me up with Gabriel Logan?"

Henry started to speak, but Elisabeth interrupted him. "The truth."

"I simply introduced two mutual friends. Faith needed a contractor. Gabe is a contractor." Henry stared at his wife. "It's not my fault that she's a single woman and he's an eligible man who reminds many people of me. Or rather, the way I used to be before meeting you."

"I don't think you've changed that much." Elisabeth sighed, leaned over and kissed Henry's forehead. "Which means we have to find a twelve-step program for Cupid wannabes."

Oh, Henry. Faith knew he had only her best interests at heart, but she hadn't left Hollywood to find another fiancé. Her shoulders sagged. "This is a setup?"

His sheepish grin was the only answer she needed. "I may have had a few ulterior motives in mind when I told you about Gabe Logan."

"The truth finally comes out." Elisabeth's skin glowed both from being out in the sun and her pregnancy. "As it always will."

But this was one truth Faith wished she'd known

about earlier so she could have prepared herself. Instead she'd almost fallen into Henry's trap. Gabriel was handsome. She couldn't deny her initial burst of attraction. Of course that had faded once she got to know him. "So what am I supposed to do now?"

"Marry Gabe and live happily ever after right here in Berry Patch," Henry suggested. "Our children can play together."

Both Faith and Elisabeth ignored him.

"You could find a new contractor," Elisabeth said. "Though Gabe *is* the best around."

But was he the best contractor for Faith? He said he wanted to help her. She was tempted to believe him. She needed his expertise. But even if she could trust him, could she trust her own judgment? Or was she making the biggest mistake of her life?

Chapter Four

At your service, milady. The dark knight knelt at Faith's feet, placing his sword at her service.

Her heart beat faster. She longed to see his face, but his lowered visor frustrated her desire. He reached up with a gauntleted hand. At last. At last...

Crash. The walls shook.

Faith bolted upright.

Earthquake? She looked for the nearest door, but the rattling stopped. She waited for another jolt, for more shaking, for a sine wave to make its way across the floor.

Nothing happened.

And then she remembered. She wasn't in the tournament stands, waiting for her true love to reveal his identity. She wasn't in Southern California, in the massive Hollywood Hills home she'd once owned. She was in Oregon. Berry Patch, to be exact. Staying in a carriage house converted into an apartment.

Faith rubbed her tired eyes. She glanced at the clock.

Seven-oh-three in the morning.

Too early, especially after a night spent reading library books about Craftsman architecture and design. She felt as if she were back in high school cramming for finals. Another hour of sleep...

Something banged, a different sound than before. This time, the carriage house didn't rattle or creak. The sound became sharper, more distinct. Hammering.

At this hour?

Realization hit like a yard of cement. The remodeling had begun.

Without her.

Faith scrambled out of bed. She'd planned to be at the house before Gabriel and his crew arrived this morning. Say eight or nine o'clock. She'd never thought they would start this early.

Faith grabbed clothes from her suitcase.

This was not the way she wanted the remodeling project to go. Not after yesterday's tense meeting with Gabriel. She'd wanted a fresh start—to wow him with her newfound Craftsman knowledge, her determination to get the job done right and the basic carpentry skills she'd learned while working on a housing project with ex-fiancé number five. But right now she felt thirty-nine steps behind.

In the bathroom, Faith glanced at the shower.

Forget about it. She didn't have time.

Five minutes later, she slipped on the work boots she'd purchased last night at Leonard's Hardware

Store. New shoes weren't in her budget, but she'd had no choice. Gabriel Logan followed the rules—his rules—and she wouldn't give him the opportunity to nail her on anything, including footwear. Even she knew canvas sneakers weren't appropriate for a construction site.

On the way out of the carriage house, she slid on a pair of sunglasses. She had stressed the importance of keeping her identity secret with Gabriel, but she wasn't taking any chances. That's why she'd created the DBA—doing business as—name of Gables Inn B and B for any paperwork involving the house, too.

Being recognized had long since lost its appeal, but more importantly she wanted to keep her project a secret from her family. When they purchased the B and B, she wanted it to be because of the restoration, not because she owned it.

On the walk to the main house, the noise level increased. Hammering, voices, a barking dog. Frank, no doubt. She shuddered at the thought of facing the long-toothed mongrel but kept walking. She feared its owner and what today might bring more.

In the driveway between the carriage house and the alley sat a blue drop box that resembled a garbage can on steroids.

"Faith."

She recognized Gabriel's deep voice immediately and turned toward the sound of her name. He stood in the front yard next to his truck. He wore shorts, a green T-shirt and a leather tool belt. A lovely dark-haired woman, in khakis and a blue knit shirt, stood next to him.

As she approached the two, Faith noticed the blueprints rolled out over the truck's hood. She couldn't help but wonder who the woman was and why she was at the house with Gabriel this early in the morning looking at remodeling plans. The more Faith thought about it, the more flustered she got. And that bothered her. Gabriel was nothing more than the guy she'd hired to remodel her house. Yet the closer Faith got to the couple, the more she felt as if she'd been nominated for a Razzie three years in a row.

She stood next to Gabriel. The scent of his soap surrounded her, making her want to inhale deeper, fuel the warmth pooling within.

Wait a minute.

So what if he smelled good? It was only his soap. Not him.

"There's someone I want you to meet," he said.

The brunette smiled. She was attractive, a cute girl-next-door type, with a clear complexion and sparkling blue eyes. She looked very comfortable, relaxed, standing next to Gabriel. The woman's identity and her relationship to Gabriel was none of Faith's business. As long as the woman didn't interfere with his ability to get the job done, Faith amended.

"You're prettier in real life," the woman said.

Oh, no. Faith's chest tightened. She'd been recognized. Sunglasses were an accepted disguise in Beverly Hills—a way of saying 'I'm not working now, please leave me alone'—but not so in Berry Patch. Maybe she would have to color her hair.

"Thanks," she said, managing a smile the way her publicist would want her to.

And then it hit Faith. What if the woman hadn't recognized her? What if Gabriel had told the woman about her? She had explained her concerns about unwanted publicity and thought he understood. This wasn't good.

Still she extended her arm to the woman. "I'm Faith Addison."

The woman returned the handshake. "Kate Logan."

Logan? Faith kept a smile plastered on her face, but inside she seethed. Gabriel was a married man and he'd asked her out yesterday. She'd been attracted to him—his smile, his scent, his tool belt—and tempted to say yes. Well, if she'd had any fantasies that he might be her knight in shining armor in disguise, she could put them to rest now.

The rat—make that the married rat.

Where was the poison? Or a hungry cat?

Okay, she shouldn't be so surprised. Faith had learned the hard way that attractive men were usually jerks, but still she felt sorry for Kate. "How long have you and Gabriel been married?"

He laughed.

The sound grated on her worse than a director's "cut" during a crucial scene. Faith's muscles tensed. She saw no humor in adultery.

"Don't mind my brother," Kate said. "He's like this sometimes."

Faith studied the two. Both had blue eyes, though Gabriel's were darker, and brown hair, though Kate's was darker. But she was more petite than Faith thought a sibling of his would be. "You're Gabriel's sister?"

Kate nodded. "Which means he's stuck with me."

"I've tried to get rid of her—" Gabriel winked "—but nothing's worked so far."

Kate punched his arm. "You'd miss me if I was gone."

The two Logans' relationship shouldn't matter, but a strange relief washed over Faith as well as a jolt of attraction similar to that she'd felt yesterday when she'd been up that tree and he'd been charming and flirtatious. Obviously he cared a great deal for his sister.

"I would miss your designs." Gabriel rolled up the blueprints. "Kate drew your remodeling plans."

"He has to keep all the work in the family." Kate grinned. "Cheap labor."

Gabriel handed the plans to Kate. "I'll remember that when it's time for raises."

"Sure you will, big brother."

The exchange reminded Faith of her older siblings, Will and Hope. Faith missed them so much. Of course, she would see them on a daily basis once she finished working on the B and B. The thought of having all this behind her brought a smile to her lips. "So Logan Construction is a family business?"

"Sort of," Gabriel said. "Bernie works on my crew, too."

"Your brother?"

"Sister. Bernadette," Kate answered. "She's finishing up another job this morning and will be by later."

"Bernie is a master carpenter," Gabriel explained. "Almost as good as—"

"You?" Faith raised a brow.

"My oldest sister, Cecilia," Gabriel said without missing a beat. "But she hung up her hammer to follow in our father's footsteps and become a farmer."

Kate, Bernie and Cecilia. Faith tried to remember the name of the sister he'd mentioned yesterday. Theresa. That was it. "So you have four sisters."

"Five." Gabriel counted off on his fingers. "Cecilia, Kate, Theresa, Bernie and Lucy."

So many sisters. One part of her envied them. Another was more realistic. Unless their house had five bathrooms, getting ready in the mornings must have been a nightmare. "Any Logan brothers?"

"No such luck. The last time my mom got pregnant we ended up with a Lucy instead of a Luke," Gabriel said. "I love my sisters, but a brother would have been nice."

"My brother felt the same," Faith said. "I'll tell him it could have been worse than just two sisters."

"A lot worse," Gabriel said. "Just so you know, Lucy is a huge fan of yours, so watch out. She's seventeen and—"

"Very sweet," Kate interrupted. "Lucy just has a tendency to get excitable and…overreact at times."

"Most seventeen-year-olds are guilty of that at one time or another." Faith had been there herself.

Gabriel studied her. "Just remember that when you meet Lucy, and don't say I didn't warn you."

"I consider myself warned."

He raised his chin. "That was almost too easy."

Sunlight hit his eyes and deepened the color to a vibrant cobalt. Faith's breath caught in her throat. There was nothing easy about this. Someone needed to warn her off him. Now.

"Everything's easy for you Gabe," Kate said. "Don't let him make you think otherwise, Faith."

Faith wouldn't, once she was able to move. She stood transfixed, frozen like a deer in headlights. Something told her she was about to become roadkill if she didn't look away. Yet she didn't—couldn't.

The moment dragged on and on...

"I'm heading back to the office now." The words rushed from Kate's mouth and broke the moment. "Nice to meet you, Faith. Later, Gabe."

Before Faith could say goodbye, Kate hurried down the street. "That was fast."

"She's always in a rush. Places to go, people to see, houses to design." Gabriel stared at his sister's retreating figure as she rushed toward Main Street before turning his attention on Faith "You're up early. Big plans for today?"

She nodded once. "I'm going to help with the house."

A beat passed.

And another.

He was going to say no. She just knew it.

She waited. And waited. Preparing herself.

Gabriel glanced at her feet.

"Sure," he said finally. "But if you're working at the site you'll need to wear a hard hat."

"O-kay." But it wasn't. Not really.

Sure Gabriel had said he would listen to her ideas and let her make the final decisions, but she'd expected a fight over this, a battle of wills. And she'd wanted to win. She needed to win.

"I have an extra one in the truck," he offered.

"Okay."

Forget eloquence, she sounded like a moron, but Faith couldn't help herself. Once again Gabriel had surprised her. Staring at his backside as he reached into the truck wasn't helping matters. Neither was his Mr. Nice-and-Charming act. Which, she wondered, was the real Gabriel? The guy she'd met by the tree, the guy who hated everything she wanted to do with the house or the guy who was so sweet to his sister?

He backed out of the truck and handed her a yellow hard hat.

"Thanks," she said.

He looked at her shoes again. "New boots?"

She tilted her chin. "Yes."

Something—respect? Humor?—flashed in his eyes. "Nice."

"Thanks."

Wow. Things were better this morning. Gabriel had taken to heart what she'd said yesterday. Maybe this would work.

"There are a couple of things we need to get straight," he said.

So much for this morning's pleasantries... She squared her shoulders. "What?"

"You mentioned staying on or under budget yesterday, but you have to understand that time is money. If you want to work on the house, you have to follow the same rules and the same standards as all my crew. If not that will cost us time—"

"And money," she said.

His gaze locked with hers. "You understand?"

She nodded and held her breath, waiting for what he had to say next.

Gabriel motioned to the house instead. "Then let's get to work."

* * *

Walking toward the house, Gabe shortened his stride so Faith could keep up with him. Already she was slowing him down, and he knew it would get worse.

Over the years, he'd dealt with enough clients who wanted to "help" to know Faith's presence on site would only cause problems and more work. But he'd held his tongue. Bit it to be exact.

If Faith wanted to help, Gabe would let her. After losing his cool yesterday, he was trying to make up ground. No way would he risk losing this project to another contractor, but he got the feeling she wouldn't hesitate to fire him if the whim appealed to her.

And whim was what this was all about.

Someone like Faith wouldn't last doing real work—the kind he planned to assign her. Someone like Faith would rather spend the day shopping or wine-tasting or having a spa day. The sooner she came to the same conclusion, the better. She might even realize Berry Patch and this house weren't for her.

"Um, Gabe? Friends of yours?" Faith asked.

He looked at the front porch. J.T., a former minor-league baseball player turned carpenter, stood at the living-room window with his gaze glued on Faith and drool practically running out of his mouth. Standing next to him was a wide-eyed Eddie, a nineteen-year-old apprentice, whose mouth gaped.

Damn. All Gabe needed were two starstruck workers. He grimaced. He couldn't afford any cost overruns, especially labor-related ones.

"I hope they are inside for a reason," Faith said.

"Yes." And Gabe paid them to work, not to stand

around gawking at Faith like lovestruck puppies. The idea of an all-female crew had never sounded so great. But unfortunately, he was stuck with these two. "J.T. is a carpenter, and Eddie is an apprentice. Good guys."

But guys. Young. Single. Cocky.

Add Faith to the mix and that equaled trouble with a capital *T.* Gabe brushed his hand through his hair.

As much as he hated to admit it, he could appreciate the sentiment. Who wouldn't want to gape at her? She looked cute in her hard hat with her hair falling loose past her shoulders. He'd expected hair and makeup to rush out any minute followed by an entourage of assistants. But it didn't happen. Her face was as natural as it had been yesterday. She was even wearing a similar pair of jeans and a white T-shirt. Not to mention a pair of steel-toed boots.

"I can't wait to meet them," she said.

He expected sarcasm from her, but didn't hear it. If anything, she seemed amused by the two men who jockeyed for prime window space. "They feel the same way."

Faith raised her sunglasses. "Do they want to meet me or Faith Starr?"

Was there a difference? On second thought, Gabe knew better than to go there. "You, of course. They know not to open their mouths about you to *anybody.*" He stressed the last word.

Still she looked doubtful. Not that he blamed her. Gabe wouldn't put it past J.T. to up his standing at the bowling alley by bragging about meeting Faith Starr.

J.T. and Eddie burst out of the house looking more as if they were auditioning for roles in a *Dumb and Dumber* sequel than professional construction workers hired to do a job.

J.T. immediately struck a pose—one that no doubt had the baseball groupies panting in Davenport, Iowa. "Hey."

Eddie's normally flushed cheeks reddened further. "H-h-hi."

"Hello." Faith climbed the porch steps toward them. "I'm Faith Addison."

J.T. tilted his head and thrust his pelvis forward in a strange Elvis Presley adaptation. "J. T. Beauchamp at your service."

"I'm Eddie." The apprentice's voice trembled. "Eddie Mallery. *In Deep Waters* is my favorite movie. When you swam with that tail and then climbed up on the boat without any clothes. I mean…"

To be young and stupid again. Gabe sighed. Not for all the money in the world. "She knows what you mean, Eddie."

"You do?" he asked.

She nodded.

Relief mixed with embarrassment. Poor Eddie.

J.T. rolled his eyes. "So if you need anyone to show you around, Faith, I'm your man."

At her service and now her man. What was he going to do next? Strip so she could examine the merchandise first? "Back to work, you two."

"Nice to meet you," Eddie stammered. "B-bye."

J.T. cocked a brow. "Later, babe."

The two disappeared inside. Good thing or Gabe might have had to fire them. "In case you're wondering, they're harmless. If they bother you, just shoo them away like you would flies."

"Flies?"

"Better than swatting them like mosquitoes."

She ran her fingertips over a piece of carved wood on the porch. "Better for who?"

He smiled.

"And I'm serious about everyone on my crew knowing you want this project and your presence to be kept quiet." Gabe wanted her gone, but he didn't want her hurt. Plus she had a point about publicity. He didn't want a distracting media circus coming to *his* town and disrupting *his* schedule. "I've threatened them if it makes you feel any better."

"It does." The doubt disappeared. Gratitude filled her gaze. "Thanks."

"You're welcome."

"Speaking of harmless, where's Frank?"

"On the porch outside the dining room. Tied up."

She touched his bare forearm, her hand soft and warm against his skin. "Thanks."

Gabe wasn't sure what he should concentrate on more. Her gratitude or the fact she was still touching him and tingles ran up and down his arm. He looked at the house and had his answer.

"No problem." He hated tying up Frank, but Gabe couldn't risk being fired over his dog. Like it or not, he had to cater to Faith's whims if he wanted to keep this job. "Frank will get used to it. Or maybe you'll get used to him."

She didn't say anything, didn't shrug, just removed her hand from his arm.

Remember the house.

"Or maybe not," Gabe added.

As the corners of her mouth lifted, his chest tight-

ened. First tingles, now this. He didn't understand. Not
when he felt as though he were tiptoeing on eggshells
and would be in worse shape than Humpty Dumpty if
one of them cracked.

Nothing could go wrong.

He had to stop feeling this way.

Faith tossed her hair behind shoulder and Gabe felt
as though he'd been punched in the gut.

And then he remembered. What he felt was normal.
The same with J.T. and Eddie. Faith was a movie star.
Okay, a former one, but she was still gorgeous with
long, supermodel hair that women would kill for and
a million-dollar smile that was probably still insured by
Lloyd's of London. Gabe wouldn't be male or breathing if he weren't attracted to her. Not attracted, he corrected. Aware of her. That's all it was. An awareness.

Now that he'd put a label on it and understood what
he was feeling, he could deal with it, make sure it didn't
impact the remodeling.

"I thought you might like to know we're already
ahead of schedule." Gabe wanted to get back to what
was really important—the house. "Yesterday afternoon, Eddie removed the fixtures and outlet covers,
grounded the circuits and covered the floors to keep
them from getting damaged."

"I didn't notice anyone here."

"My entire crew was in and out," Gabe said. "You
were gone."

Two lines formed above the bridge of her nose. "Oh,
I had a late lunch with Henry and Elisabeth. And I
stopped by the library."

"For what?" Gabe asked.

"Books." She stepped onto the tarp-covered floor of the foyer, looked around the living room and screamed. "What have you done? It's ruined."

The anguish in her voice sent every one of his nerve endings on alert. J.T. and Eddie ran in from the dining room.

"Back to work," Gabe ordered and luckily they listened to him. He didn't need those two adding to this disaster. Not when he had to do some serious damage control.

"We're in the demolition phase."

"*Demolition* is the correct word." She stared at the lath and plaster from one of the exposed walls. "You're supposed to remodel the house, not destroy it. It looks as if a bomb went off in here."

Damn. This was his fault. He should have warned her. "You're right. It does look like a bomb exploded in here. I should have explained that this place might resemble a war zone rather than a home. In most cases, we're not really remodeling a house, but rebuilding it."

She touched an exposed two-by-four. "The walls are gone."

"Remodeling is more than patching and painting," he explained, feeling as though he was the one about to be torn down if he didn't get this right. Still he kept his tone light, tried anyway, and motioned to a partially demolished wall. "Take this over here."

She followed him.

"These walls are lath and plaster. They are cracked and need to be replaced along with the pipes and electrical wiring inside them." He paused to see if she was getting it or not. From the look on her face, not.

He tried another tack.

As he explained what they'd done, he still didn't see any relief settle over Faith's stunned expression. Gabe felt as if he'd just poured quick-set cement at the wrong house. But he wasn't giving up. Not until Faith understood why the living room looked like this and why the rest of the house would, too.

"And so you see, this is the cheapest way to do it," he concluded.

Her sharp gaze met his. "The cheapest?"

He nodded. "And the best."

"Oh."

Gabe waited for her to say more, to define whether "oh" was a good thing or a bad thing. Faith said nothing. She simply adjusted her hard hat, picked up a mallet and smiled. "We're wasting time just standing around. Show me what to do."

He saw a determination in her eyes he hadn't noticed before. A strength. A challenge.

Maybe there was more to her than just being a beautiful, pampered actress playing in his house. And if that were true, getting Faith out of here wasn't going to be as easy as he'd hoped.

Chapter Five

"Great job, Faith," Eddie said from the sunroom doorway.

As Faith dropped the final pieces of lath and plaster into the wheelbarrow, dust flew up, getting her even more dirty than she already was. For once, she wasn't the movie star or the little sister. She was nothing more than a member of Gabriel's crew expected to pull her own weight.

With a gloved hand, she removed her mask. "Thanks."

"No, thank *you*." Eddie's grin widened. "We're ahead of schedule and it's because of you."

Pleasure warmed her. She was sure she'd done a couple of things wrong, and she'd broken a piece of molding, but Faith had surprised herself with the amount of work she'd accomplished. She hadn't realized others had noticed, too.

"Really?"

"Really."

She smiled. The week had flown by in a blur of plaster dust and demolition. Five days of swinging a mallet and hauling debris from the house had just about wiped her out. Her muscles and back ached. Scrapes and scratches covered her arms. Only her borrowed gloves kept her hands from blistering. But Eddie's words suddenly made all the effort worthwhile. "Then I better get back to work."

"Me, too—" Eddie glanced behind him "—before the boss man catches me and thinks I'm slacking off."

She raised the handles of the wheelbarrow and made her way down the ramp to the backyard. Sweat trickled down her back and dampened the tendrils around her face. Just her luck—a heat wave had hit Oregon this week. What she wouldn't give for some nice, cool rain...

Wheeling the debris to the drop box, she glanced at the dining-room porch. Frank lay in the shade on a blanket with bowls of food and water nearby. The dog stared at her—his sad eyes blaming her for his being tied up—but he didn't sit up or bark. Still she steered in a large arc away from him, doubling the distance she needed to travel. She didn't care about the extra work it took if it meant avoiding Frank.

After emptying her wheelbarrow at the drop box, Faith sat on the front-porch steps. She pushed back the hair stuck to her forehead and guzzled from an icy-cold water bottle. Tired and sore, yes, but she welcomed the work.

The house still looked as if it would qualify for disaster-relief funds, but she now understood why and had contributed to the mess. Her body might suffer from the manual labor, but her pride swelled with the accomplishments.

She placed the water bottle against her cheek.

The porch creaked. The nuances of the house had become second nature. She didn't have to look up to know someone stood behind her or who that someone might be.

Faith lowered the water bottle from her face. "I finished in the sunroom."

"That puts us ahead of schedule."

No compliments or atta boys from Gabriel Logan, but she respected his work ethic and determination to get the job done right. She no longer doubted his being the best contractor for this project. Faith had learned more from him on her first day working here than she had after an entire weekend of building and fixing up low-income housing with fiancé number five.

Gabriel sat next to her. "How are your hands doing?"

"Fine," she said. "Thanks to Elisabeth's gloves."

"Can I have a look at them?"

His question surprised her. Once Gabriel showed her how to do a job, he kept his distance, occasionally checking to make sure everything was okay, but nothing more. No idle chitchat, no eating lunch with her and the other crew, nothing but business.

And that was fine by her.

"Sure." No doubt he wanted to maintain a work schedule and would show the same concern with any member of his crew. If she hurt herself she couldn't work. Faith set her water bottle on the step and showed him her hands. A little dirty and wet from the water bottle, but no blisters. "See?"

Gabriel's brows furrowed. "Do you mind if I take a closer look?"

"Uh, okay."

He examined the palms of her hands and each of her fingers one by one. As he ran the pad of his thumb over her hand, his calloused skin felt rough against hers, but his touch was soothing, reassuring. His tenderness surprised her.

"Your hands are okay, but you need to be careful."

Faith nodded.

She needed to be careful all right, but it wasn't her hands she was worried about. Being so close to Gabriel sent her nerve endings, heart rate and breathing into spasms. Or maybe it was just the heat. She moistened her lips.

"Or take a few days off," he suggested.

"Am I not pulling my weight?" she asked.

"You are, but—" he brushed his hand through his hair. "Blisters aren't fun."

They might be if *he* took care of her. Strike that. "That's what Elisabeth said when she loaned me these gloves. She told me what happened to Henry's hands when he first started working on the farm."

"Did she tell you about the bees?"

The laughter lacing his words intrigued Faith. Smiles from Gabriel were rare commodities. He acted so serious on the job site, the flirtatious rescuer she'd met that first morning at the tree nowhere in sight. Until this glimpse of him now.

"No," she said.

"Ask Henry about the bees."

"I will." She glanced down and realized Gabriel still held her left hand. The gesture felt so comfortable, so right that she hadn't even noticed. Had he?

Trying to control the heat flooding her cheeks, she pulled her hand away, reached for the water bottle and downed the rest of its contents.

Gabriel seemed unaffected. Faith must be overanalyzing this and making it bigger than it really was. Darn. She wanted to leave her drama-queen days behind her in Hollywood.

"You spend a lot of time over at Henry and Elisabeth's," Gabriel said.

It wasn't a question. How did he know where she spent her evenings?

"They have that new hot tub," Faith said. "That helps my muscles feel better."

"Have I been working you too hard?"

She didn't want him to think she was complaining. She didn't want to give him an excuse to kick her off the crew. "It's just a different kind of work than I'm used to."

"You could install a hot tub here temporarily."

Maybe once when she was rich and famous. Now that she was poor and infamous, a metal tub and a garden hose were more in line with her budget. "I don't just go there for the hot tub. I like being around the kids. Plus eating takeout alone every night would get old fast."

"You should go out," Gabriel suggested. "See the town."

Faith would love to explore Berry Patch. To check

out The Vine, a local tavern the crew talked about. To taste the berry cobbler at the corner bistro. To have a hazelnut chocolate milkshake at the creamery. But she didn't want to risk being seen. "I will eventually."

She would once the house was finished and sold to Starr Properties, when being recognized would no longer matter since her family would no longer be in the dark about what she'd done. Of course, that was weeks, if not months away. She picked at the water bottle's label with one fingernail, reluctant to meet Gabriel's eyes…reluctant to move away.

"How about tonight?" Gabriel asked.

She glanced up at him. Her pulse skittered.

"Tonight?" she forced the word from her dry throat.

He nodded. "Are you going to Henry's?"

"I haven't spoken with them yet."

"You can't stay home alone on a Friday night," Gabriel said. "You need to go out, don't you think?"

Oh, my. He was asking her out again. Her toes curled. She'd been tempted to say yes the first time. Now she wanted to say yes.

But could she? Should she?

"I…" Feeling tongue-tied and thirteen again, she fumbled for the correct words. If only she had a script…

He smiled, accentuating the lines around his eyes. "You know you need a break."

Faith wanted to sigh. Instead, she nodded feebly. Pathetic, but she didn't care.

"Good." His smile widened, and a sigh escaped her lips. "I know Henry and Elisabeth would love to show you around town."

Henry and Elisabeth?

Faith's heart plummeted to her feet, through the porch staircase and into the earth's core.

It wasn't a date. Not by a long shot.

She swallowed a strange and sudden disappointment. "On second thought, going out wouldn't be a good idea."

Gabriel raised a brow. His eyes seemed to see into her soul. "Why not?"

Because I wanted to go out with you.

The safest place for her was the carriage house or the Wheeler Berry Farm. Anywhere she could be away from Gabriel Logan. Thank goodness she had another excuse. "I could be recognized."

"You've already been recognized."

"What do you mean?" Panicked, she glanced around for the photographers hidden in the bushes or behind cars. No whirring of helicopter blades filled the air. "I haven't been away from the house except to grab dinner or drive to Henry's. And I always wear a disguise."

"You always wear jeans and a white T-shirt."

"Camouflage," she explained. "Pictures of me wearing jeans and a white T-shirt have already been published. If someone snaps another picture of me in this outfit, it will be worthless because no one will be able to tell when it was taken. That's why I always wear something like this. I have a bunch of the same shirts and jeans. Stars do this all the time when they want to grab a cup of coffee or go shopping."

"I had no idea."

"Of course, if someone photographed me doing something outrageous, then the press would want the pictures."

"Outrageous?"

"Kicking a dog, getting arrested, that kind of thing."

"Well, the fine citizens of Berry Patch don't know that and a few of them have recognized you."

"When?"

"While you're working, sitting out here, eating lunch." He motioned to the street. "Check out the traffic."

A few cars drove by the house, slowing as they passed. "That's not traffic."

He chuckled. "It is for Berry Patch."

Faith scooted up the stairs to the porch and sat with her back to the street. "How did they find out?"

Gabriel rose and stood on the porch. "I don't know, but I let it be known you want your privacy."

That brought relief, but was it enough?

Her family thought she was staying at a friend's ranch near Telluride for an extended vacation. If word reached them about the B and B... "Do you think telling them that is enough?"

He shrugged. "Folks in small towns tend to look after their own."

Hope started. "You mean they consider me one of them?"

"I wouldn't go that far," he drawled. "More like you're Berry Patch's own private celebrity. They don't want to share."

"You mean I don't have to hide?" she asked. "I could go into a restaurant to eat and not just order takeout?"

"I can't promise word won't leak out, but I don't see much point in you parading around in recognizable disguises or pretending to be somebody else."

He had a point.

"So will you?" Gabriel asked.

She didn't know why he was so interested in having her seeing more of the town.

"Will Faith what?" Bernie stepped out of the house. Her baggy denim overalls were covered with white powder from the wall plaster, and her yellow T-shirt had seen better days. Her gelled-back hair was pulled into a ponytail. If not for her feminine voice, high cheekbones and small hands, she could have passed for a guy. "Is my big brother bothering you?"

"No, he was just telling me I should go out tonight."

"You should," Bernie encouraged. "The Vine is the place to be on Friday nights. Come with us."

"Us?" Faith asked.

"Me, J.T. and Eddie," Bernie explained. "We always cut out of work early on Fridays, head home, shower, then meet at The Vine for dinner. They have burgers and beer on special."

"Faith isn't interested in going to The Vine," Gabriel said.

"Actually," Faith countered, "I am. Henry told me about it. Sounds like an interesting place."

"Great." Bernie grinned. "It's walking distance for you. On Main Street just past the bank."

Gabriel's lips thinned.

"Too bad you can't join us, bro." Bernie jabbed him in the arm. "Gabe reserves Friday nights for hot dates."

Hot dates. Faith wasn't surprised. What woman wouldn't want to go out with him? She wondered what he considered "hot."

Not her, that was for certain.

Until looking at her hands today, he'd barely noticed her. Once upon a time, before the press had dubbed her as flighty, flirty and fickle, she had been considered a hot date. A hot everything. Some men, such as J.T. and Eddie, might even think she was still hot. But Gabriel...

"It's not even close to quitting time," he said to Bernie. "Don't you have stuff to do?"

"What is wrong with you?" his sister asked. "I hope Sally gives you what you need so you can get back to normal."

As Gabriel glared at Bernie, Faith tried not to imagine what Sally would be giving him tonight.

"Faith," Bernie said. "I'll tell J.T. and Eddie you'll be at The Vine. We're usually there around five-ish."

"Don't walk home alone if it's too late," Gabe said.

Faith stared at him. "We're in Berry Patch, not in L.A. or New York."

"Things can happen anywhere," he said. "Even in Berry Patch. But don't let J.T. walk you home alone. Have Eddie do it."

"You sound just like my big brother, Will," Faith said. "Is this how you are with your sisters?"

"Worse," Bernie said before disappearing back into the house.

A muscle ticked at Gabriel's jaw.

A smile tugged at the corners of Faith's mouth. "Don't worry, I'll be careful tonight."

"And stay away from J.T."

Okay, the gruff tone was uncalled for. Faith should just let it go... No, she shouldn't. "You think?"

Lines creased Gabriel's forehead. "Think what?"

"That I should stay away from J.T." She was baiting Gabriel, but she couldn't help herself. It would give him something to think about on his hot date. No, she realized, it wouldn't. Still she wasn't about to stop now. "J.T.'s kind of cute in a rampant, testosterone-out-of-control kind of way."

"He's young and stupid."

"Trainable."

Gabriel's nostrils flared.

Faith tried not to laugh. Boy, she was glad she wasn't one of his sisters. "I'd better get back to work so I can cut out early to get ready for my big night on the town."

He said nothing, simply stared at her as she walked toward the front door. Halfway there, she turned. "And Gabe?"

"What?" he asked.

"You be careful tonight, too."

"I'm not a woman walking home alone."

"No," she said. "But I wouldn't want you to get burned on that hot date."

"What were you thinking?"

That afternoon Gabe unloaded hay bales and stacked them in the barn at the Wheeler Berry Farm. He hadn't been to the farm since Faith arrived. Nor had Henry returned any of his phone calls.

Henry Davenport sat atop his sparkling John Deere tractor and buffed it with a chamois cloth. "You think I should have bought a Kubota?"

"Forget about your new tractor." Gabe lowered his voice in case Elisabeth, her brother or two sisters were around. "I'm talking about Faith Starr."

Henry looked down from the tractor. "What do you think of her?"

"She's not as tall as I thought she would be." Sweat trickled down Gabe's back. Heat? Or her? Earlier he'd wanted to convince her construction work wasn't for her. Instead he'd ended up holding her hand and almost asking her out on a date. For someone with a reputation for being smooth, he sure wasn't handling this well. "Why the hell didn't you tell me who F. S. Addison was?"

"She asked me not to."

"I'm your friend."

"So is she." Henry went back to buffing. "Would it have made a difference?"

Gabe took a swig from a water bottle. Faith might not be as prissy and pampered as he had once thought a star would be, but that didn't change the most important fact. "She doesn't belong in Berry Patch."

Henry concentrated on a spot that didn't shine as brightly as the rest of the tractor. "Faith Starr might not belong here, but Faith Addison does."

"She's one and the same."

"You know her that well already? After what—a week?"

"That's long enough to know."

"Know what?" Henry asked.

Gabe scuffed the toe of his boot in the dirt. "Stuff."

"Aw, right. The all-important 'stuff.'" Henry glanced at him. "She told me it was going well."

"She would think so."

"And you?"

He shrugged. "It could be worse."

And it could. Faith could want wall-to-wall carpet and pink walls. She could want to paint all the trim white and add skylights to every room. Yes, it could be much worse than her just wanting to put in a solid-day's work. Maybe he was being a little too harsh on her. Gabe picked up another hay bale.

"I've never seen a woman have you so riled before." Henry studied him. "Shot down?"

Gabe dropped the bale. "That was before I knew who she was."

"Are you going to try again?" Henry asked.

"No way."

"Why not?"

"Let's see…she's a movie star, she bought my dream house out from under me, and she's turning it into a B and B." Gabe tensed. "What would we talk about? How she wants to screw me next?"

"That could be interesting." Henry climbed off the tractor. "I'm sorry about the house, Gabe. If I had known you wanted it, I would have never told Faith about it."

Gabe picked up the bale and placed it on the stack. "I know."

"To make up for it, I've figured a way for you to get the house back."

"I'm listening."

Henry smiled. "Marry Faith."

Gabe's jaw sagged. "Are you crazy?"

"It's a good idea."

"It's a stupid idea." Gabe knew what he needed in a wife. "Have you lost your mind?"

"It was there the last time I looked. Though Elisabeth

might tell you differently," Henry said. "You and Faith would make a striking couple. And your children would be beautiful." His chest puffed. "I could be their godfather."

Leave it to Henry. Gabe rolled his eyes. "So I'm just supposed to ask one of the most famous, beautiful, sexy women in the world to marry me so I can have her house?"

Henry nodded once. "After you date her and fall in love, of course."

"Of course," Gabe said with as much sarcasm as he could manage. "I thought Elisabeth made you promise not to play matchmaker anymore."

"I'm not." Henry buffed a spot on the tractor. "I'm only helping two friends."

"Stop helping. Please."

"Why?"

"Lots of reasons."

Henry glanced at him. "Tell me one."

"I have plans."

"Plans?" Henry asked.

"Plans for the future." Gabe rubbed the back of his neck. "She doesn't fit into them."

"You aren't building a house," Henry said. "You can't live your life according to a blueprint."

"I have so far."

And Gabe was proud of it. He wouldn't end up like his father. Gabe had his life all planned out. Only one person—Faith—stood in his way of getting what he wanted.

"What else?" Henry asked.

"Someone like Faith Starr wouldn't want to stay in Berry Patch."

"Someone like you doesn't have to stay here."

"It's home," Gabe said, his tone harsher than he intended. "I don't want to live anywhere else."

Henry shrugged. "Then the only thing left for you to do is buy the house from Faith."

"Like she's going to sell it."

A Cheshire-cat grin lit up Henry's face.

Gabe's heart slammed against his chest. "She's going to sell the house?"

Henry nodded.

"Why? When?"

"That's up to Faith," Henry said. "I've probably told you too much already."

Excitement almost robbed him of speech. "I won't say anything."

And Gabe wouldn't.

His dream wasn't dead. All he had to do was convince Faith to sell the house to him. That would take some effort and possibly a lot more cash depending on the results of the remodel. He'd have to start watching expenses, his own and the project's. But that would be easy with such a prize in sight.

He'd also have to be nice to her. Real nice.

It wouldn't be that hard. Not when he considered her enthusiasm. Her excitement. Her smile. Her body.

Yeah, it wouldn't be hard sucking up to a beautiful woman if he remembered what was at stake.

Once Faith left Berry Patch, he would have the house. He already had the dog. The only thing missing would be…a wife.

Chapter Six

Forget the hip, trendy nightspots in L.A. and New York, Faith preferred The Vine. The hole-in-the-wall bar was exactly as she had imagined it and movie-set perfect—a dark, windowless interior, peanut shells strewn across the beat-up floor and the scents of hot grease and beer hanging in the air.

Faith leaned back in her chair and shoved another French fry into her mouth. Diets weren't allowed in a place like this. Cigarette smoke, either, thanks to a town-wide smoking ban spearheaded by Berry Patch's Mayor Logan, who also happened to be Bernie and Gabriel's mother.

The best thing about The Vine, however, was its customers. People filled the tables and crowded at the bar, but no one ventured to the back room where she,

Bernie, Eddie and J.T. sat. No one had asked for her autograph. No one had taken her picture.

A perfect night. Faith crossed her fingers under the table. So far.

J.T. stared at her over his mug of beer. "Are you sure you don't want to see my balls?"

Bernie rolled her eyes. With some eye shadow, eyeliner, lipstick and a sleeveless blue blouse with bootcut jeans, she had transformed herself from tomboy to knockout. "Subtle J.T., real subtle."

He raised his chin and eyebrows. Faith wasn't sure what facial expression J.T. was going for—desire, perhaps?— but he looked as if he were in pain or constipated. She pressed her lips together to keep from smiling.

"I appreciate the offer, J.T., but I'm not really into baseball collections." Faith placed her glass of water on the table. One beer had been more than enough for her. She might not be in the spotlight any longer, but she knew better than to lose control. "Now if you had any autographed hockey pucks…"

His grin disappeared; his forehead wrinkled. "Hockey pucks?"

"I grew up in Lake Tahoe," Faith explained, feeling for the first time in a long while that she could open up without fear of being sold out. It was hard not being able to trust anybody. "Everyone skied, snowboarded or played hockey. My friends and I were partial to hockey players."

Bernie winked. "J.T. is too much of a pretty boy to have ever played hockey."

"I like hockey," Eddie said, one of the few times he'd

said anything all evening because he'd been eating so much—three hamburgers, an order of fries and a side of onion rings. Not to mention the beer. Shaggy and Scooby-Doo could take lessons from him. How Eddie stayed so slim mystified Faith. If only she knew the answer, she could share it with women everywhere...

J.T. picked up the half-empty pitcher of beer and refilled everyone's mug except Faith's. "No way am I going to put my body—my temple—or my face in jeopardy playing hockey."

Bernie snickered. "That would be such a loss to all of us."

He ignored her. "But all this hockey talk has made me realize something."

Eddie leaned over the table. "What?"

"I have finally figured out why Faith doesn't find me irresistible."

"This should be interesting," Bernie mumbled.

Faith agreed. J.T. might be a bit over the top with his women-can't-help-but-want-me bravado, but she sensed there was more to him than that. "And why is that?"

"Because you like men with mullets, broken noses and no teeth." J.T. flashed her a devilishly charming grin. "See, I have all my teeth."

Everyone laughed. It had been a long time since she'd had this much fun.

"Oh, no—" she covered her heart with her hand and tilted her head back "—my secret is out. Promise you won't tell."

Eddie's eyes darkened. "Would someone pay for that information?"

Faith dropped her glass on the table. Water spilled, but the glass didn't shatter.

"Eddie," Bernie scolded and reached for a napkin to wipe up the water.

J.T. thumped Eddie on the head. "You moron."

Country music played on overhead speakers. Someone shouted a greeting in the main room. One pool ball struck another.

Time to go. She pushed her chair back and started to rise.

Bernie placed her hand on Faith's arm. Compassion filled the young woman's eyes. "He didn't mean it."

"It's better if I go," Faith said. "It's getting…late."

"He's only kidding, Faith." J.T. glared at Eddie. "Aren't you?"

Red-faced, Eddie nodded. "I—I'm sorry, Faith. I wouldn't tell anyone. Not ever. Not even for—"

"A million dollars," Bernie finished for him.

"You're safe with us," J.T. added, his bravado disappearing in sincerity. "Even if you like hockey better than baseball."

Faith appreciated their words. If she wanted to keep the evening from being a total bust, she would have to believe them. Yet suddenly she wasn't so sure. About anything.

Still she wanted a life, a real life with real friends who didn't even know what being A-list meant. She didn't want to hide out, wear disguises, be someone she wasn't.

"Please stay," Eddie said. "Gabe told us how much you wanted all of this kept secret. Man, if he found out what I said, even as a joke, he'd kill me. I'm too young to die. I've never even had a girlfriend."

As J.T. rolled his eyes, Faith sat. "I wouldn't want to be an accomplice to murder."

Eddie released a huge sigh. "Thank you."

"I'm really sensitive about my privacy," she explained.

"After Rio Rivers, I can imagine," Bernie said.

Faith cringed. Not Rio. Again.

Bernie covered her mouth with her hands. "I'm so sorry, Faith. I shouldn't have brought him up."

"It's okay." And Faith realized it was. These people weren't going to sell her out. They were the closest things to normal friends she'd had in almost ten years. "That was nothing compared to what happened after our breakup."

"I saw it," Eddie admitted.

"He shouldn't have proposed on camera," Bernie said. "Live, no less. My youngest sister, Lucy, was livid."

"At least I wasn't the only one," Faith said.

"She was furious and so worried about you." Bernie toyed with her napkin. "And now she's mad at Gabe."

"Why?" Faith asked.

"Lucy wants to meet you, but Gabe laid down the law and won't let her near you."

Gabriel's protectiveness sent a warm and fuzzy feeling washing over Faith. "I don't mind meeting her."

"She's only seventeen," Bernie said. "She'd be expecting Faith Starr, not Faith Addison."

"That's okay."

"Wow. That's so nice of you." Bernie smiled. "And I know the perfect place. Why don't you stop by my niece's first birthday party on Sunday? That would be the perfect time. Lucy won't be able to totally monopolize and annoy you."

"Lucy won't annoy me."

"We'll see about that," Bernie said.

"Are you sure it's okay if I come?"

She nodded. "It's in Kate's backyard. Nothing fancy. Barbecue. Cake and ice cream. Balloons."

"Sounds perfect." The description reminded Faith of the pictures from her nieces' and nephew's first birthday parties.

"Knowing Kate, it will be perfect. Her daughter, Annelise, is the apple of her eye." Bernie motioned to J.T. and Eddie. "These two will be there."

Faith laughed. "Then how can I say no?"

"Lucy will just die. She really is one of your biggest fans." Bernie's eyes sparkled and Faith appreciated what this woman wanted to do for her younger sister. "Lucy even gathered names on a petition and sent them to Rio Rivers demanding he retract his proposal and publicly apologize."

"Now that is a true fan," Faith said.

"I'm glad she did it. I would have signed it. Proposing like that was very uncool," J.T. added. "And totally unromantic."

"That's really perceptive of you, J.T." Bernie stared at him. "I didn't know you had it in you."

He shrugged, but sat a little straighter.

"Rio's sweet," Faith admitted. "But young."

J.T. cocked his head. "I'm sexy, but young."

Young was the operative word. She could no more be romantically interested in him than in Eddie, but she appreciated him sticking up for her. "You know, J.T., you could be the perfect man for me, but..."

He leaned over the table toward her. "But what?"

She gave him a big sigh and an even bigger smile. "You don't play hockey."

Bernie and Eddie laughed. J.T. joined in.

Eddie drew his thin brows together. "Didn't Gabe—?"

"Did I hear my name?" a familiar voice asked behind Faith.

She turned.

Gabriel stood in the doorway with a pint of beer in his right hand. He wore a blue polo shirt and jeans. Not exactly dressed-up, but the clothes suited him. He looked...nice. Okay, he looked hot. But that was only because he had a hot date. Speaking of which, where was she?

"What happened with Sally?" Bernie asked.

"She got a last-minute call. A bridal party needs hairdos in the morning so she wanted to call it an early night after dinner and get to bed."

"And you're here because...?" J.T. asked.

Faith wanted to know the answer to the question, too. Cutting short a date was one thing, but that didn't explain why he was here or why he kept looking at her as if she were the last box of chocolate candy at the movie snack bar. She expected such a look from J.T., but not from Gabriel.

She hadn't expected to see him until Monday morning. That would have been soon enough for her. Not that she didn't like him. She did, a little too much.

Faith had seen enough this week to know Gabriel

Logan was a hardworking, reliable contractor, a caring brother and dutiful son. But he wasn't exactly the chummy boss type, the kind of boss to join his employees for lunch or beers after work. At least not with her on the crew.

"I wanted a beer," Gabriel answered.

The others accepted his answer. Faith wished she could do the same, but something was different about him. He seemed happier. Maybe dinner with his hot date had made the difference.

"It's been a while since I joined you all here on a Friday night," he added.

Bernie cleared a space for him. "Pull up a chair, bro."

As he sat next to Faith, his solid thigh brushed hers.

"Sorry," he said.

"That's okay." But it wasn't. Heat spread from the point of contact. She tried to scoot over, but the table was too crowded. Obviously one beer had been one too many. She needed another glass of water.

As J.T., Eddie and Bernie argued about the Seattle Mariners' latest trade, Gabriel placed his hand on the back of Faith's chair. She inched forward on the seat to avoid him touching her again.

As if reading her mind, Gabriel picked up the water pitcher and refilled her glass. "Having fun?"

She nodded. "I needed to get out."

And right now she wanted out of here. Tension, once again, charged the air. Only it had nothing to do with the wrong thing being said. It had to do with Gabriel Logan. The temperature had risen at least ten degrees. The air seemed thick, dense. She found it difficult to think straight.

"I hope you'll get out more," he said.

Her brain just couldn't function. She nodded again.

"Faith's going to be a regular with us here at The Vine," J.T. announced.

"I am." She forced the words out. Her tongue felt heavy, her mouth dry. She gulped water. It didn't help.

"Didn't you used to play hockey, Gabe?" Eddie asked.

Faith nearly spit out her mouthful of water. She tried not to choke.

"Yeah, a little," Gabriel said.

"A little?" Bernie snickered. "Gabe was the center on the top line in college."

Impressive. Faith sure wouldn't want to go up against him on a face-off.

He set his glass on the table. "Why did you want to know?"

"Faith has a thing for hockey players," Eddie announced, then glanced around. "But you can't tell anybody, okay?"

"My lips are sealed." Mischief gleamed in Gabriel's eyes. "Why hockey players?"

Faith didn't want to answer his question. What she really wanted to do was crawl beneath the peanut shells on the floor and hide. Instead she swallowed around the puck-size lump in her throat. "Gotta love a guy with a mullet cut and a big stick."

Gabriel laughed. "I can't do much about the haircut…"

J.T. snickered. "What about the big stick?"

Time to change the subject. Faith did not want to think about Gabriel's stick. "Why don't we play darts?"

He stood. "Great idea."

J.T. and Eddie rose and made their way to the dart-board.

"Let's split into teams," Gabriel said. "Faith and I against the three of you."

Everyone nodded. Everyone except her.

She didn't want to be on his team, didn't want to be a part of his "us versus them." She liked having Gabriel as her contractor, she enjoyed working on Gabriel's crew, but she wanted to keep things on a strictly business basis with him.

Playing darts on a Friday night was safe; playing darts as Gabriel's teammate wasn't.

He motioned for her to join him. "Come on, partner."

Partner? Faith hung back. It was bad enough he had wanted to look at her hands earlier today, brushed her thigh with his when he arrived and put his arm on her chair after he sat. She couldn't imagine what he would do next. The knots in her stomach would make Master and Commander Aubrey proud.

"Is something wrong?" he asked, looking genuinely concerned.

Oh, yes. Something was definitely wrong. Rather than tell him the truth, she forced her wanting-to-stay-stuck-to-the-floor feet to move. She expected someone to shout "dead man walking" as she approached the others.

It was only a game of darts, she reminded herself.

So what if Gabriel Logan wasn't like all the gorgeous men who had come before? So what if he was more than just a pretty face? She was immune.

He placed darts on her palm and covered them with his hand, searing her skin. He moved closer, real close.

"Let's show them we've got the right stuff," he whispered, his beer-scented breath warm against her neck.

She found herself nodding.

Immune, remember?

Gabriel grinned, his eyes full of anticipation. "Bring it on."

Faith gulped. A booster shot to increase her immunity might not be such a bad idea.

Gabe always believed Faith Starr to be dangerous, but until tonight he'd never known how right he was. The woman kicked butt playing darts. Good thing she was on his side.

"We win again," he announced to the moans and groans of the other team.

Bernie plopped down onto a stool. "You guys are unstoppable."

"No kidding. I'm not used to losing," J.T. said. "I need another break. Winners buy this round."

Faith reached into her back pocket and pulled out cash, but Gabe wouldn't take the money she offered. "I've got it covered."

"Bernie?" a feminine voice called.

Bernie straightened. "Mom?"

"What are you doing here?" Gabe asked. Their mother never came to The Vine. She always referred to it as that smelly, dark place and wrinkled her nose whenever he mentioned it. "Is anything wrong? Dad?"

"Your father's at the bar telling Hal about his plans to farm algae or something like that. All I know is it's green." With a Queen Elizabeth wave, his mother greeted J.T. and Eddie. Veronica Logan liked being one of Berry Patch's VIPs and upholding a polished image of what a mayor in a small town should be. After she had survived the chaos and uncertainty of raising six children and never knowing when money would arrive or where it would come from, Gabe didn't blame her for wanting to take control of Berry Patch and its future.

Becoming mayor had fulfilled a half-century dream of his mother's and saved her marriage. She was a planner married to a man who didn't know how to spell the word *plan*, let alone know its definition. Now she didn't have to worry so much about her husband and the farm. She focused on her six children, her five granddaughters and Berry Patch.

"What are you doing here, Gabe?" she asked. "I thought you had a hot date with Sally."

"Change of plans."

"Just like us," Veronica said. "We had dinner at the bistro and were on our way to the creamery when we saw The Vine. I thought we should stop in and say hi to Bernie. I always know where she is on a Friday night."

Bernie groaned. "Mo-om, that makes me sound pathetic."

"No, just predictable." Veronica smiled. "Now we get two hellos from our children when we thought we'd only get one. How lucky is that? Maybe I should buy a lotto ticket. Berry Patch could use the extra taxes, you know. If I could only figure out a way to up revenues…"

Gabe loved and respected his mom, but they'd heard enough at dinner on Sunday about her economic plans to turn Berry Patch into the Willamette Valley's version of Napa and Sonoma. He didn't want to get her started again.

He glanced at Bernie, who motioned to Faith, standing in the corner near the dartboard. He nodded.

"Mom, have you met Faith Addison yet?" Bernie asked.

"Faith Addison?" Veronica asked. "Well, hello there. I'm Veronica Logan, Berry Patch's mayor."

Despite her desire for privacy, Faith extended her arm with practiced charm. "It's nice to meet you."

His mother's polished smile curved into a canary-eating grin. "The pleasure's all mine."

Suddenly her appearance at The Vine made perfect sense to him. She'd known Faith was here. Not good.

Gabe glanced at the front room. No strangers that he could see. Good. That meant no press. He'd already spoken to Paul, the editor of the *Berry Patch Gazette,* and warned him to keep Faith's secret.

"Have you seen much of the town?" Veronica asked.

"A little," Faith said.

Her voice sounded so controlled; her posture was stiff. Her face was blank and polite. Her public persona? Gabe didn't like it. Not after seeing her at ease playing darts and joking with the crew.

"Your son has me working hard on the house."

"That's right," Veronica said with nonchalance, but the gleam in her eye told Gabe she was anything but indifferent. "Fred Taylor told me you bought the Larabee Mansion."

Faith wet her lips. "Fred?"

"Taylor," Veronica said. "He owns the only garage in town. Nice man. Knows everybody's business."

Faith smiled tightly. "Guess he knows mine."

"Don't worry, dear," Veronica said. "He can be discreet."

"He'd better be," Gabe said.

"Well, I'm sure your father has talked Hal's ears off." Veronica reached into her jacket pocket and pulled out a business card. "If there's ever anything I can do for you, Faith—a referral to a hairdresser or the key to the city—please don't hesitate to call."

Faith took the card. "Thank you."

Uh-oh. His mother was up to something. She never did anything without a reason. And if it involved Faith...

"I need to buy another round for everybody, Mom," Gabriel said. "I'll walk you out."

"Nice meeting you, Mayor Logan," Faith said.

Veronica waved. "See you around town."

Once they were out of the back room, he pulled his mother aside. "Faith doesn't want anyone to know what she's doing here."

"Everybody already knows."

"Only people in Berry Patch."

"So she wants to avoid publicity?"

He nodded. "It would be a mess if the media found out."

"Then we'll just have to keep it our little secret." His mother glanced at the back room. "I can see why you've been complaining about your new client. She seems sweet, but a bit uptight."

"She's not uptight."

Veronica pinned him with the same look she'd given him the time he'd stuck a banana up Mr. Gessel's exhaust pipe. "And you know this how?"

"It's complicated."

"I have five beautiful daughters and a drop-dead gorgeous son," Veronica said. "I understand complicated."

"She's been helping out at the job site."

"That explains the complaints." Veronica smiled. "At least she's pretty to look at."

No, Faith Starr was beautiful, the lone piece of mahogany in a pile of plywood, but he wasn't about to admit that to anyone, especially his mother, who wanted more grandchildren. "If you like that type."

"You don't?"

"She's a client, Mom. Nothing more. I doubt she'll stick around once the job is finished," Gabe explained.

"Why is that?"

"She's a movie star, Mom. She doesn't belong in a place like this."

"This happens to be a nice place."

"For us, but not for her."

His mother's eyes widened. "She said that?"

"Let's just put it this way." Gabe motioned to Hal for another pitcher. "The sooner she leaves Berry Patch, the better for all of us."

"Six games to zero," Gabe said to Faith as he walked her home from The Vine. Streetlights illuminated the cracked sidewalks. In the distance he heard the bank's clock chime midnight. "No one came close to beating us."

Faith shoved her hands into her pockets. "We should have changed teams."

"And lose? Forget that."

"What about playing fair?" she asked.

"I like to win."

"I never realized you were so competitive."

"It just depends on what's at stake. Tonight it was bragging rights." He glanced at the Larabee house and stopped. "Damn."

"Something wrong?"

"It looks like a light's on upstairs."

"It could be the moon."

"Or a halogen work light. Those things get real hot." He stared at the room. "I need to check it."

"I'll come with you."

When they reached the porch, he stopped. "It's dark inside. You could fall."

"What about you?"

"I know the floor plan of this house better than the house I grew up in. Okay?"

"Okay," she said.

"Don't move. I'll be right back."

He unlocked the door and entered the house. He'd been wrong about it being too dark. Moonlight shining through the windows lit his way to the staircase.

Upstairs, he walked down the hallway and entered the far bedroom. Faith had been correct. It was the moon, not a halogen work light. Shadows from the framed walls made a grid pattern on the tarps covering the hardwood floors. He stood for a moment and listened to the breaths of the house—creaking and settling. He also heard…footsteps.

"Gabriel?" Faith called out. She was in the house, not on the porch. "Are you okay?"

"I'm fine."

"Do you need help?" she asked.

"Not unless you know how to turn off the moon."

"Never learned that one."

"Then we'll just have to leave it on. I'll be right down."

He found her standing next to the fireplace in the living room. Moonlight glowed softly and surrounded Faith. The gentle light magnified her beauty. He'd never seen anything more lovely, more perfect in his life.

Her gaze met his. "Even with all this mess, I see the potential now."

He felt a tugging at his heart and took a step closer to her. "Good. So do I."

She took a step toward him. "Yes, good."

Another step. And another.

"What are we doing?" she whispered.

The closer they got, the less sense any of this made. "I don't know.

"This probably isn't a good idea."

He closed the distance between them. "Probably not."

She bit her lip. "I should get back to the carriage house."

"You should."

But she remained standing amid the moonbeams and shadows.

Gabe cupped the left side of her face. Her skin was as soft as his was rough. Logic told him to stop. Common sense told him he would regret his actions. He didn't care.

He tilted her face toward him. One taste. That was all he wanted. He lowered his lips to hers and found…home.

Warmth and sweetness and completion.

One taste wasn't enough, but did he dare take more?

Hell, yes.

He pulled her closer and she went eagerly, her mouth pressing against his with urgency. Her response surprised him, pleased him. Warmth became heat. The sweetness intensified. And completion—only one thing would complete him now. Blood roared through his veins. His temperature soared.

She wove her fingers through his hair, trailed kisses along his neck, murmured his name.

When he captured her mouth again, her breasts pressed against his chest. The rapid beating of her heart matched his. Her lips parted and Gabe's control evaporated.

Stop.

Logically that was what he should do, but Gabe was beyond rational thought and action. Everything he'd been searching for his entire life was suddenly right here in his arms. He hadn't felt this way in years. Not since his ex-wife, Lana.

Reality hit like a wrecking ball. Faith wasn't sticking around Berry Patch, either.

Gabe pulled back. When Faith followed, he placed his hands on her shoulders. "I'm sorry."

"For kissing me or for stopping?"

He stared at her. Wide-eyed. Swollen lips. Flushed cheeks. She looked the way he felt—kissed inside and out. Desire surged.

"Stopping. No, kissing. I... Oh, hell—" he brushed his hand through his hair "—I'm just sorry. Okay?"

"It's not okay."

"Excuse me?" he asked.

"I said it's not okay," she repeated. "I kissed you back."

"I started it."

"Why?"

"Why what?"

"Why did you kiss me?" She bit her lip. "I mean, this entire week you've treated me like an employee or a little sister. Tonight, you stared at me as if I was a new tool that you just had to have. And now you just kissed me. What's going on?"

He hadn't expected this response from her. Under normal circumstances, he might have admired her directness. Now it made him feel awkward and defensive. "Do you always question people's motives?"

"It's something new."

"Lucky me."

"Look, I've been burned one too many times," she admitted. "This project is too important to me to let a kiss get in the way of anything. So I need to know."

"What?"

"What do you want from me?"

Everything she had to give. No, Gabe realized with a start. What he wanted was the house.

Her house.

And only that could explain his kissing her tonight. The truth made him feel as worthy as dry rot.

"What, Gabriel?" she pressed.

"Nothing."

She flinched.

He didn't want to hurt her. "I'm sorry."

"You already said that."

"But it's true." He couldn't afford to upset her, to allow this kiss to ruin all he hoped to achieve. "I am sorry. This has all been a mistake."

"A mistake." Her voice sounded flat.

"Yes, a big mistake." He gazed into her eyes and noticed the spark was missing. "Can you forgive me, Faith?"

Forgive him? Faith wanted to smack him.

She increased her stride to get to the carriage house faster. Anything to get away from him.

"Wait," Gabriel called after her.

Let him chase her. Better yet, let him fall on his face chasing her. She wasn't about to stop and listen to anything more he had to say.

She'd wanted answers. Answers that might explain why she'd gotten carried away and kissed him back, but all he offered was a lame apology about how kissing her had been a mistake.

A mistake.

Gabriel was correct.

Kissing had been a huge mistake, but it wasn't only his mistake, it was hers, too.

Darn. No, damn.

This was serious.

After making so many mistakes already and vowing to change, she was right back where she'd started. Only this time it was worse. Gabriel wasn't just a good-looking guy she'd misjudged. He had the power to ruin her plans, her future.

"Faith. Please."

With trembling fingers, she inserted the key into the carriage house's lock and opened the door. Before she could slam it closed, his hand stopped it.

"I said I was sorry." His gaze implored her. "It was only a kiss."

For him maybe, but for her…

Faith's heart had melted with his kiss. Her lips still tingled, wanting more and more. In Gabriel's arms, she'd felt a sense of belonging she'd only dreamed about. A place she wanted to return to again and again. His embrace offered security, warmth, acceptance.

But she didn't belong in his arms or anywhere near him. Berry Patch and the Larabee Mansion were merely a means to an end.

"Yes, it was only a kiss," she said finally, more annoyed with herself than with him. "If I could take it back, I would."

She expected—wanted—a reaction from him, but didn't get one.

"So would I," he said, almost sounding wistful.

Faith ignored the disappointment seeping through her. "At least we agree on something."

One corner of his mouth curled upward. "We agree on a lot more than that, Faith."

Those were the last words she wanted to hear because she knew they were true. They'd agreed to put their differences about the house aside and work together. But unfortunately she knew there was more to it than that. She frowned.

"Hey, don't be like that." He rocked back on his heels. "What can I do to make it better?"

Kiss it better.

No, that was the last thing she wanted, needed.

Disappear so I never have to see you again.

No, then who would remodel the house? Despite everything, she still believed he was the right man for the job. Which put her in an awkward position. She thought for a moment and came up with a solution.

"You can stop apologizing and never mention it again. We have to keep working together so it's best if we pretend it never happened."

How pathetic. She couldn't even say the word *kiss*.

"Fine," Gabriel said. "Anything else?"

"I want you to treat me like I'm one of the crew."

"That's what I've been doing all week."

"So you kiss Bernie, J.T. and Eddie, too?"

"Point taken. Anything else?"

"Nothing else." She folded her arms over her chest.

She waited for him to say "no" or to tell her to quit or to take her in his arms and kiss her again.

"Okay," he said.

"Okay," she repeated.

But it wasn't.

She'd gotten exactly what she wanted, yet she didn't feel that overwhelming sense of relief. If anything, she felt empty.

"And Faith?"

She took a deep breath. "Yes?"

"See you at six-thirty Monday morning." He took a step away from her. "Don't be late."

Chapter Seven

Gabe was late. He'd rather not have shown up at all, but he wasn't going to miss his niece's first birthday party.

He parked his truck in Kate's driveway.

At least he had Annelise's present ready, and it was perfect. His fifth dollhouse for his fifth niece. He'd stayed up all night putting the final touches on it. Not that he could have slept anyway. Images of Faith's long hair, thoughtful gaze and generous smile appeared in his mind each time he closed his eyes. Memories of that hot, amazing kiss had kept him awake two nights straight.

Lust? Guilt? More likely a bad case of stupidity.

Gabe turned off the ignition.

He'd spent almost half his life working toward a dream, but if he kept messing up around Faith, he would lose the Larabee house again and only have himself to blame.

Frank whined.

Gabe glared at the dog sitting on the passenger seat. "Don't you start on me, too."

He'd been fielding calls from his sisters all weekend. They wanted to know all about Faith Starr, but it was more than curiosity about a famous actress when the questions turned personal. Did he like her? Did she like him? He didn't know what to say to them. Hell, he didn't know what to say to himself.

Gabe set his jaw. Enough about her. He slid from the truck, unloaded the dollhouse and carried it into the house. Today was for Annelise.

He returned to the truck to get Frank. As they made their way to the backyard gate, the scent of marinated chicken grilling filled the air. Gabe's stomach growled.

As he opened the gate, Frank nudged between his leg and the fencepost. Suddenly high-pitched squeals and screams drowned out the Wiggles song playing on the boom. Cecilia's daughters—Savannah, Madeline, Anna and Danielle—raced up and flung themselves at Gabe and Frank, showering man and dog with indiscriminate sticky-fingered hugs and wet kisses.

Their unconditional greeting warmed Gabe's heart. He glanced over the tops of their heads and searched for his sisters. Pink and purple balloons were tied everywhere. Lawn chairs had been placed on the grass. A buffet table sat on the covered patio.

On the far side of the yard, he found them. Rather, some of them. His mother, Theresa, Bernie and Lucy stood in a semicircle in front of the picnic table. None of them had noticed his arrival. Good. He wanted to avoid an interrogation at all costs. No doubt his mother would be worse than his sisters since she hadn't called him all weekend.

Kate strolled over to hand him a bottle of root beer still wet from the cooler. "Hey, bro. Did you finish the dollhouse?"

At least she wasn't asking him what time he'd left Faith's on Friday night; Bernie had. He smiled. "It's in the living room with the other presents."

"I can't wait to see it." Kate smiled back. "Annelise is going to love it."

He unscrewed the bottle cap and took a swig. "Where is she?"

She motioned to the picnic table. "Over there."

Annelise wouldn't let just anyone hold her—so far only Kate and Gabe's dad had been honored with that privilege. If someone else tried to hold her, Annelise scrunched up her face and screamed until she turned red.

"With Dad?" Gabe asked.

His father watched Annelise during the week if Kate had to be at a job site or meet with a client.

She grabbed a diet soda from the cooler. "Dad's in the kitchen with Cecilia."

"Then why isn't Annelise screaming her head off?"

"My daughter is too enamored to scream."

Not even Gabe, who had charmed almost every female young and old in Berry Patch, had succeeded in holding Annelise without crocodile tears shooting from her baby blues. "I don't believe it."

"See for yourself." Amusement glimmered in Kate's eyes. "I need to put the bread in the oven."

Gabe would pass for now. His mother and sisters had ways of getting him to talk. He wasn't about to walk into an ambush. He hit the buffet table instead and popped one of Theresa's stuffed mushrooms into his mouth.

Frank, wearing a pink Happy Birthday cone hat and purple streamers, trotted by. The girls followed him.

"Come on," J.T. said, stepping out of the house with a soda in his hand. "I haven't wished baby Annelise happy birthday yet."

"You did so." Eddie grabbed a potato skin off the table. "Right after we arrived."

"Well, there were so many people around her, she probably didn't hear me."

"Yeah—" Eddie glanced at the picnic table and the women surrounding it "—she probably didn't hear me, either."

Without so much as acknowledging Gabe's existence, the two walked across the grass toward the picnic table.

Something was going on, and Gabe didn't like being the only one left out. He tossed his empty bottle into the recycle bag and squared his shoulders.

Time to face the inquisition. Maybe with whatever it was distracting them, he'd get off easy.

As he neared his mother and sister, peals of baby laughter floated on the air. Annelise sounded like a normal, happy baby—the way she sounded only in the comfort of her mommy's arms or on her grandfather's lap.

Lucy stood next to Bernie and blocked Gabe's view of the table. "I can't believe how happy Annelise is."

"I know," Bernie said. "She never acts like that when I hold her."

Lucy nodded. "Me, neither."

Curiosity got the better of Gabe. He peered over Lucy's shoulder…

Faith?

For the first time, she wasn't wearing jeans and a white T-shirt. She wore a floral print dress instead. His heart jolted. Attraction rippled through him.

No. He'd spent all weekend trying to drive her from his thoughts. He didn't need her showing up in his sister's backyard at his niece's birthday party.

What the hell was she doing here?

Resentment overflowed. She didn't belong here.

Still Faith, a movie star and about as far removed from what a perfect wife and mother should be, held his niece. A bit awkwardly from the looks of things, but Faith wasn't cringing at the drool or the hair-pulling or the openmouthed kisses. Instead she sang, a sweet lullaby about mermaids and pink elephants. Annelise clapped her chubby, dimpled hands and grinned.

But she wasn't the only one smiling at Faith. His mother and his sisters smiled at Faith as if she'd discovered the secret to zero-calorie, no-carb desserts. Not once in the three years he and Lana had dated during high school or during their one-year marriage had his family smiled so acceptingly at his former wife. Not that Lana had ever tried earning their acceptance.

He remembered when his cousin, MaryAnn, had given birth to her first child. Lana had wanted nothing to do with the newborn. She'd paled and nearly passed out the first time the baby spit up. His family never brought babies near Lana again.

Yet with Faith Starr, they'd handed over the youngest member of the family as if they were giving her a pet to hold, rather than a baby.

Gabe felt as if he'd been smacked in the head with a two-by-four. Couldn't they see she didn't belong here?

"It's amazing, Faith," Bernie said. "You can swing a mallet like a pro, throw darts like a champ and soothe babies like a horse whisperer. Is there anything you can't do?"

"I haven't changed that many diapers."

"Cecilia can help you there," Theresa said.

Faith shifted the baby on her lap. "I don't know how to use a nail gun yet."

J.T. took a step forward. "I can teach you that."

Eddie careened into him. "No, I can."

Ah, man. Gabe brushed his hand through his hair. Faith had enamored every single one of them.

"Dammit," he said.

Every pair of eyes focused on him, including Faith's.

His mother tsked. "Watch your language around the children."

"I need some help with the buffet table, Bernie." Gabe pulled his sister away. "Come on."

"Does Kate want it moved?" Bernie asked.

"The table is fine." Gabe glanced at the picnic table. He wasn't sure who people fawned over most—Annelise or Faith. "What is Faith doing here?"

"I invited her."

"Why?"

Bernie beamed. "To meet Lucy. You know what a big fan she is. Did you know Faith brought a present for Annelise?"

Nothing Faith did would surprise him.

"This is a *family* event."

Faith might get along with everybody this afternoon, but she would never fit into his family. She was leaving town soon. He wanted her to leave. He wanted her house.

Bernie studied him. "J.T. and Eddie are here."

"They work for me." His raised voice drew stares from across the lawn.

"Faith works for you, too," Bernie whispered.

"Technically we work for her." Gabe gritted his teeth. "J.T. and Eddie belong here. Someone like Faith doesn't."

"That makes zero sense, bro."

Nothing about Faith made sense. That was the problem. "Lucy's probably driving Faith insane with her badgering."

"Lucy hasn't badgered once," Bernie said. "Only mild fawning and hero-worshipping. You'd be impressed."

Gabe wasn't.

"Oh, my gosh. You won't believe this." Lucy ran up. Her cheeks flushed; her eyes twinkled. "Faith offered to run through my lines with me. Faith Starr helping me, Lucy Logan, rehearse for a part in the community play. Is that cool or what?"

Lucy flitted inside.

Gabe crossed his arms over his chest. "She's only going to cause problems."

"Lucy?"

"Faith."

Bernie pursed her lips. "Friday night, you sure sang a different tune. You couldn't get enough of Faith with that buddy-buddy partner, teammate trash talk. You weren't worried about problems then."

"I should have been."

"I know you said you went right home after you walked Faith to the house—" Bernie raised a brow "—but did something happen between the two of you?"

A beat passed. "No."

"Yes, it did." Her eyes widened. "What did you do?"

"Nothing."

"Liar." She tapped her cheek with her finger. "You kissed her good night, didn't you?"

Gabe knew Bernie was only guessing, but how did his sisters always figure these things out? His mother, too? He hated their interest in his personal life. And this time his motives wouldn't stand up to their scrutiny.

He made an exaggerated sigh. "What are you talking about?"

"Don't pretend with me, Gabe Logan." Bernie placed her hands on her hips. "Women know these things."

"Women might, but tomboys don't."

"I'm only a tomboy on the outside," Bernie said. She waved. "Hey, Faith."

"Hi." Faith's smile looked forced as she walked up to them. "Hello, Gabriel."

The way she said his name made him stand straighter. *Idiot.* He hunched a shoulder and noticed her empty arms. "Where's Annelise?"

"She started to get fussy so Kate took her."

"Annelise must be hungry," Bernie said. "You're a natural with her."

A natural? Gabe stared at Faith. Maybe if she were playing the role of a mother in a movie.

"I'm not a natural," Faith said to his surprise. "I haven't spent a lot of time with babies."

"Aren't you an aunt?" Bernie asked.

Faith shrugged. "I used to travel a lot."

Of course she traveled, Gabe realized. She was a movie star. That's what they did. They had houses everywhere, not just one place to call home.

"Would you like something to drink?" Bernie offered. "A soda? Champagne?"

"No, thanks." Faith drew a deep breath. "I should probably go."

Bernie's forehead creased. "It's almost dinnertime."

Faith glanced at him, and Gabe realized he was the reason she wanted to leave. A part of him was relieved, but the other part felt like a jerk.

She didn't deserve to spend tonight alone at the carriage house eating takeout because he felt uncomfortable. He was thirty-two years old, not twelve. And he wanted her to like him, or at least tolerate him. Having her annoyed with him wasn't going to get him the house.

"Stay," he said. "Kate's planned a big spread."

"Cecilia made her famous chocolate cake," Bernie added.

Faith's indecisive gaze bounced between them. "I—"

"Oh, Faith, here you are." Kate appeared with a

wriggling Annelise in her arms. "Would you mind holding the baby for a few minutes? I need to do a few things in the kitchen, so we can eat and my dad's gotten sidetracked in the garage."

As Faith took Annelise, the baby greeted her with a wet, openmouthed kiss.

Better Annelise than me.

"Does this mean you're staying?" Bernie asked.

With a rueful smile, Faith shifted the baby in her arms. "Looks like I've been drafted."

"Good." Bernie smiled. "I'd better go see what my dad's doing in the garage before he breaks something."

Faith watched her enter the house. "I hope this isn't too…awkward for you. I'd totally forgotten about Bernie's invitation until she called with directions this morning."

Had something else been on Faith's mind? Their kiss? Gabe shouldn't want to know. He didn't want her here, but he wasn't about to be rude. If she could be gracious, so could he.

"It's okay." But after he said the words he realized it wasn't. All this felt…wrong. If he didn't know better, he'd think his sisters had manipulated this entire situation. But no one could have gotten Annelise to accept Faith—a total stranger—so easily.

Doubt filled her eyes.

"I mean it." He held out his hand and Annelise tugged on his little finger. "And Kate's happy to have someone else hold the baby besides my dad. She's had a tough time, but the sparkle is back in her eyes tonight. You had something to do with that."

"Bernie told me about her husband drowning in that

boating accident. My brother, Will, lost his first wife in a car crash. They didn't have any kids, though." Faith paused. "It took him a long time to find a woman who could convince him to give love another try."

"Kate is too focused on making sure Annelise has what she needs to worry about what Kate needs."

"Give her time."

"I know." Gabe tapped the tip of Annelise's nose. "But this little one deserves to have a daddy who loves her."

"This little one might not have a daddy, but she has lots of people who love her." A soft smile formed on Faith's lips. "Especially you. I heard about the doll-houses you built for each of your nieces, how you never miss a performance or event at school and how you coached Madeline's T-ball team after her dad got deployed overseas."

Annelise stuck her left thumb in her mouth and cuddled against Faith's chest.

Enjoy, little one. Gabe experienced a stab of jealousy for the one-year-old. If only he could settle into the same spot. He yanked his thoughts back, embarrassed. "Sounds like my sisters gave you a list of my best qualities."

"They tried."

He should have known. Gabe sighed.

"I'm kidding." Faith grinned. "No list, but Theresa did tell me how you followed her to make-out ridge and embarrassed her to death by flashing a million-watt spotlight in the car."

Gabe rolled his eyes. "It wasn't a million watts. Theresa was younger than Lucy, but every bit as impetuous, and dating a total loser. Make-out ridge was the last place she needed to be."

"Theresa said you were indignant about it." Faith laughed. "I can imagine how you'll be when your nieces are old enough to date. Or when you have your own daughters."

When, not if.

"I'm only having sons," he decided at that moment. He'd never be able to deal with some rutting teenager feeling about his daughters the way he felt about Faith. "But none of my nieces will be allowed to date until they are thirty. I'm going to build a tower and lock them away like they do to princesses in fairy tales."

"What if one of your princesses escapes?"

"I'll bring her back. She won't be able to pull anything over on me," Gabe said. "I know how guys think and with five sisters, I know how women think, too."

"What am I thinking?" Faith challenged.

The look in her eyes sent heat pulsating through him. The kiss. She was thinking about their kiss.

No. That couldn't be right.

Not after what she'd said to him Friday night.

But he wouldn't forfeit. He would guess.

"You think my sisters and nieces are either the luckiest females in the world for having me in their lives or the unluckiest."

"Sorry, but you're wrong."

"Close?"

"Not even." She held Annelise's tiny hand. "Don't worry, princess, your uncle Gabriel doesn't know everything after all."

He kissed the top of the baby's head. "Yeah, but I give good hugs and kisses."

"You do." Faith's cheeks flamed. "I mean, I'm sure you do."

The silence magnified the tension between them. His muscles bunched.

Each time he messed up around her, the Larabee house slipped further from his grasp. Losing the house meant kissing his dream of the perfect life goodbye. Sure he could find another house, but it wouldn't be the same. The knowledge twisted inside him. "I'm so sorry, Faith."

"No more apologies." She pressed her lips together. "I thought I made that clear Friday night."

"You did. But this was my fault."

Again.

She wanted to forget about their kiss, but he kept throwing it back in her face. What was wrong with him? And how would he make it up to her?

If the Logans knew how little experience Faith had around babies, they would have never left her sitting on the living-room floor with Annelise.

But for some unknown reason the Logan family trusted her with their youngest member. She wouldn't let them down.

"Look at the lights, Annelise." Faith pointed to the working sconces on either side of the fireplace in the dollhouse. "See the lights?"

The baby cooed.

Annelise liked her. A lot. The baby's attention flattered Faith, but she figured at any moment the baby would scream and it would all end. Until then, she could pretend she fit in. Heaven knew, even with doubts about what to do with the baby, she fit in better here than with her own family.

And that worried her.

She wanted to keep her relationship with Gabriel strictly business, but she was being pulled headfirst into his world.

Into his family.

She should fight it at least a little.

"What am I going to do, baby?"

Annelise's "goo" sounded more like "go."

"If only it were that easy, sweetie."

Leaving would be a retreat. Perhaps a wise one, but she wanted to stick it out. She wanted to show the Logan family she could handle Annelise. Maybe she wanted to prove it to herself, too.

"Guess we're in this together, baby," Faith said. "Just you and me."

Annelise toyed with strands of Faith's hair, then yawned.

"You've had a busy day. Presents, cake, a bath. And they even let me help wash you," Faith whispered.

A bath in the middle of the party had become a necessity after Annelise had smeared cake everywhere. She looked more like a giant cupcake than a baby with all that icing.

But, as Kate reminded everyone, that's what first birthdays were all about. And the impromptu bath gave Faith a crash course in baby washing.

Fear had nearly paralyzed her when Kate asked if Faith wanted to help bathe Annelise. Somehow Faith had managed to clean the baby and get herself wet in the process. Messy, but fun.

She took a whiff of Annelise's hair. This must be the baby-smell fix her mother always talked about.

A lump of regret lodged in her throat. Faith hadn't spent as much time with her nieces and nephew as she should have. Gabriel seemed to know exactly what a great uncle should do, but Faith had failed completely at being a good aunt. Not once had she made a first birthday, not once had she given any baths. She'd been too busy with her film career, her fiancés and wedding plans. No longer. Once the B and B was remodeled and sold, she would make up for her absence in her nieces' and nephew's lives. Not with presents, but with presence.

Being with the Logan family reminded Faith what family was all about—Sunday picnics, family birthday parties, potlucks. Her childhood had been full of similar memories, and she longed for that family connection again. Soon she'd be back where she belonged. Soon, she'd be home.

Home.

That was her goal, what she wanted more than anything. She'd made the mistake of looking for it in the wrong places with the wrong men, but she knew better now.

Faith glanced around the modest but comfortable living room with its hand-sewn valances, basket of toys and a plastic slide. A part of her still wanted…this. A heavy feeling settled in the center of her chest.

Annelise reached inside the dollhouse and pulled out a stuffed kitty. "Ca-a."

"Yes, cat." Faith forced a smile. "Cat."

"*Cat* was her first word." Gabriel walked into the living room carrying a slice of chocolate cake on a plate. He sat on the other side of the dollhouse and raised the dessert. "A peace offering."

"For what?"

"For apologizing one too many times."

If she accepted the cake, she would be agreeing to a truce. They had to work together, so they needed to get along. She just didn't like the way her pulse quickened whenever she saw him.

"What do you say?" His gaze held her. "You don't want to miss out on one of Cecilia's chocolate cakes."

"It looks delicious." So did he. To distract herself from her wandering thoughts, she said, "The spread tonight was amazing and everyone seemed to have brought a dish. Does all your family cook?"

"Everyone except my mother. She couldn't be bothered with anything domestic. Not back when she tried to help my father with the farm and not now with running Berry Patch."

Annelise chewed on a piece of Faith's hair and she removed it from the baby's mouth. "That must have been hard for you."

"I gave up trying to make my parents fit my idea of a perfect family a long time ago."

Faith stared at the portraits on the mantel and walls. Home, family, love. "This looks pretty perfect to me."

And it was something she'd resigned herself to never achieving. Finding her one true love and having a family of her own wasn't possible. She'd tried, several times, and failed, leaving a trail of five ex-fiancés for her ill-fated efforts. The truth squeezed her heart.

He shrugged.

"What is perfect to you?" she asked.

He took a deep breath and exhaled slowly. "A big house, a wife, lots of kids and a dog."

"Frank?"

Gabriel nodded.

Her heart had softened a little toward the giant canine after seeing him play with Cecilia's daughters. Not many dogs would put up with what those girls did to Frank.

"Sounds exactly like your family," Faith said, not wanting to admit it sounded perfect to her, too.

"I guess." He handed her the plate.

She stared with longing at the cake, especially the balloon made with pink icing. "Frosting is one of my weaknesses."

"Then why aren't you eating it?"

"I can't eat until my hands are free."

"Such a sacrifice on behalf of the birthday girl." He scooped a forkful of cake and held it in midair. "How about a taste to tide you over?"

His gaze met hers. Faith's heart beat triple-time. She tightened her arms around the baby and tried to muster strength. No way could she allow Gabriel to see the effect he had on her.

He grinned. "Open up."

Bad idea, but Faith parted her lips anyway. Slowly he placed the plastic fork in her mouth. She closed her mouth around it and took a bite. The cake dissolved on her tongue.

Gabriel pulled back the fork. "How is it?"

Awkward. Sweet. Delicious.

"Perfect." Faith licked her lips. "Thank you."

He raised the fork again. "Want more?"

Yes, but more would be a really bad idea. "I'd better not."

"Are you sure?"

She wasn't sure of anything anymore.

Gabriel Logan presented temptations far more dangerous than a few extra calories. She couldn't deny how he made her feel—alive, beautiful, desirable. Faith knew better than to rely on her instincts when it came to men. She couldn't afford to make another mistake.

But, she wondered, gazing into his eyes, would it be a mistake? Or could she have stumbled onto something unexpected and…special?

Chapter Eight

He'd come for her. Her one true love had finally come. She had been alone for so long, imprisoned and hidden away from the world.

The dark knight climbed through the tower's window. Tall, strong, hers.

As he knelt at her feet, his armor clanked against the stone floor. He had braved dangerous dragons and a treacherous climb up a wall of thorns to rescue her. *At your service, milady.*

Her heart slammed against her chest. She clutched her hands together.

He raised his lowered visor, revealing a strong chin. Firm jaw. Full lips.

She trembled. At last she would see…

The alarm buzzed, sending Faith scrambling for the off button. She stared at the clock. Six-fifteen. She had to be over at the house by six-thirty. No time to hit the snooze button. Once again, her knight would have to wait.

Instead of heading to a set to have her hair and makeup done, she was going to work on her own house—her own B and B, she corrected—and she'd never felt so satisfied.

A few minutes later, Faith found the crew sitting on the porch.

"Gabe brought coffee." Bernie raised a cup. "And donuts."

Eddie picked up a Boston cream. "Something must have brightened his weekend."

"Faith?" J.T. opened the lid to the pink box. "What's your poison? Chocolate raised, chocolate cake, glazed, French cruller, bear claw?"

She climbed the porch stairs and looked into the box. "Decisions, decisions."

"The chocolate ones with extra sprinkles are tasty," Gabriel said.

Faith glanced over. He stood at the front door with a cup of coffee in his hands. He wore long shorts, a long-sleeved T-shirt and a tool belt. Her mouth went dry. Maybe she needed something to drink rather than eat.

"Though Frank's partial to the maple bars," Gabriel added.

The dog sat at the far end of the porch with a long donut hanging out of his mouth. He took a bite, and it was gone.

She gulped. "Let's save the maple bars for Frank."

The dog barked.

Faith flinched, her reaction automatic from years of being afraid of dogs. After seeing Frank with the girls, she knew he wouldn't hurt a fly. Still she was going to keep her distance.

Gabriel stepped from the doorway so he was between her and the dog. The tenderness of his gaze made her stomach tingle. She felt a shiver of awareness.

"Frank just wants another donut," Gabriel said. "He won't hurt you."

What about you? Even with the rest of the crew right here, his nearness disturbed her, awakened something deep within her. She focused on the box of donuts.

"Here, boy." J.T. tossed the dog another maple bar. "Savor it for a minute, will you?"

Faith reached for a chocolate donut with sprinkles, but took one with nuts instead. She didn't want Gabriel to think she was picking a donut because of him.

Pathetic. She had to be nuts for thinking he would notice let alone care about her donut selection.

She took a bite.

Gabriel smiled. "I like the ones with nuts, too."

Faith swallowed. Hard.

"So now that you've all eaten, are you ready to get to work?" Gabriel asked. "I want to stay ahead of schedule."

Bernie smiled. "Now I know why you brought us breakfast, bro."

"It's a bribe to make us work hard," Faith said.

He leaned back against the wall. "Your paycheck should be enough to do that."

"I get a paycheck?" Faith smiled, finished the rest of her donut and brushed her hands together.

"Breakfast is over," Gabriel announced. "I want Eddie to finish in the attic. J.T. upstairs. Bernie, you're in the kitchen."

As those three went to work, Faith wiped her mouth with a paper napkin. "What about me?"

"You're with me today." Gabriel's eyes met hers. "I'm going to teach you how to use a nail gun so you can help us with the framing. Ready?"

Not trusting her voice, she nodded.

"Let's go."

She followed him inside to the living room. On the floor lay a nail gun, hose, a compressor, strips of nails, wood and a pair of safety glasses.

"This is a framing pneumatic nailer." He picked up the nail gun. "It can drive ring- and smooth-nail-shank nails in four gauges and has depth adjustment."

Faith took a deep breath. "I have no idea what you just said."

"It means you have to be careful or you can get hurt." He handed her a pair of safety glasses. "First, you always have to wear goggles. If I see you without them, I'll dock your pay."

"I pay you."

"Then you can feed Frank."

She would be sure to wear her safety glasses. She noticed he wasn't wearing any. "Why aren't you wearing glasses?"

"Because I'm the contractor."

"You mean a man." She rolled her eyes. "You still could get hurt."

"I never get hurt." He motioned to all the equipment on the floor. "I've already unloaded everything, but you would need to bring in the compressor and figure out what length of hose you'll need. We keep the air hoses in the truck."

"Got it."

"The nailer isn't powered by electricity but air. The air compressor is powered by electricity so you need to plug it in. This switch on the side sets the pressure." He turned it on and the noise filled the room. "Next you need to connect the air hose to the compressor."

She nodded. This didn't look too hard. Faith appreciated the care he took to make sure she understood how to use the nailer well. No wonder Bernie teased him about being Mr. Responsible. But being responsible appealed to Faith in more ways than one.

"The male end of the hose goes into the female connector of the compressor like this." He demonstrated, then took it all apart and turned everything off. "You try."

She did everything, but couldn't get the air hose to connect to the compressor. "What am I doing wrong?"

"Male connector into female connector."

Oh, boy. She focused on the hoses, but got confused.

"Let me help you." Gabriel covered her hands with his. She stared at the large hands over hers, conscious of where his warm skin touched hers.

"Got it now?" he asked.

"No." She hadn't realized he was showing her how to do it again. Heat rose in her cheeks. "C-could we try it once more?"

They did. Until she could do it with her eyes closed.

"I—I think I've got it now."

He removed his hands slowly. "Good."

Not so good. She wanted him to keep touching her. And that was very bad.

He explained how to load the strips of nails that reminded Faith of staples and how the safety trigger worked.

"Now I want you to use the nailer." He handed her the nail gun and moved a piece of wood toward her. "Hold on tight and fire into this piece of wood."

She pulled the trigger. "Ow!"

"Are you okay?" The concern in his voice warmed her heart. He really cared about her safety.

"I'm fine." She shook the sting from her hand. "You weren't kidding when you said to hold on tight. That thing really has a kick."

"Let me help you get the feel of it."

He stood behind her and put his arms and hands over hers. Her muscles tensed.

"Relax," he whispered into her hair.

Easier said than done. His warm breath fanned her neck, the scent of chocolate and candy sprinkles filling her nostrils. Great. First he'd made her mouth so dry she'd needed a drink. Now he'd made her hungry. But she wanted more than donuts to satisfy this craving.

"Fire the trigger."

She did.

"Better?"

"Much." Her body relaxed against his. She felt his heart beat against her back.

"Want to try again?" he asked.

Faith nodded. She had no desire to leave this position anytime soon. Having his arms around her felt familiar and safe. But that made no sense. This was about learning to do the job right. Nothing else.

"You are determined to succeed, aren't you?" he asked.

She fired again. "Yes."

"I admire that about you, Faith." He backed away and smiled. "You've got it."

And she wanted it, wanted him. Badly. Uh-oh.

Over the next few weeks, demolition finished and the framing was almost completed, opening the way for the plumbers and electricians—subcontractors Gabe had worked with before—to update the plumbing, heating and electrical systems. The project remained ahead of schedule and under budget. He couldn't believe how smoothly everything had gone so far. Gabe hoped this meant his entire plan would work out, as well.

It had to be a sign that Faith was working out better than expected. He liked having her around and helping with the work. Her touches made the house better. Faith wanted to turn it into a B and B, but she'd made the house a home. She admired every step of the process and exclaimed over every detail. She'd been an apprentice, interior designer and cheerleader all rolled into one.

He saw Bernie sitting on the kitchen floor surrounded by tools. "Where's Faith?"

"Upstairs finishing the honeymoon suite closet." Bernie glanced up. "Why?"

"We're going to Portland to look at tiles."

She raised a brow. "Tiles, huh?"

"At Pratt and Larsen."

"Sure, bro." Bernie grinned. "Enjoy your date."

"We're going shopping for tiles."

"You said that before." She winked. "Have fun."

What was Bernie trying to imply? This wasn't about him and Faith. This was for the house.

Gabe took the stairs two at a time.

Bernie must have a loose screw somewhere if she thought he and Faith were a couple. Yes, he and Faith had been getting along well, but that was because of the project, nothing else. They were both committed to remodeling the house. Naturally that gave them extra time to interact, but dating? Besides lunch and a few breakfasts, they never ate meals together. And Friday nights at The Vine were for the entire crew, not just the two of them. Dating? What a joke.

On the landing, Gabe saw Faith working at the far end of the house. She wore jeans, a white T-shirt and a pair of safety goggles, and she held a framing nailer in her hands. The sound of the nail driving into the wood echoed through the floor.

Attraction hit fast and hard. He'd gotten used to the burst of physical attraction he felt whenever Faith was around. He knew how to manage it and better yet, how to ignore it. Like now.

She lowered her arm, a satisfied smile on her lips.

He'd put that smile on her face by teaching her how to use the nail gun. He could think of other things to teach her that would put the same look of satisfaction on her face.

She glanced his way and waved.

"Ready to go?" he asked.

She raised her safety glasses. "Where?"

"Portland," he answered. "To look at the antique reproduction tiles. I showed you that catalog."

"I forgot that was today." She glanced around. "Can we afford the time away? We don't want to fall behind."

He appreciated her dedication to the job, but she had been working so hard. She deserved a break, a treat so to speak. And so did he. Hers was shopping, and his was…her. "They close at five. It's okay. The rest of the crew will still be here."

"Oh. Okay." She smiled. "It sounds like fun."

Her emphasis on the word *fun* set off his internal warning bells. Suddenly a two-plus-hour round trip alone with Faith didn't sound so smart. But it was only for the house, he rationalized. They really needed to get the tile. No matter what Bernie said, this was not a date.

Faith set the safety on the nail gun, placed it on the floor and disconnected the air hose.

Downstairs, she grabbed her keys. "I need to get my purse and sunglasses from the carriage house."

"My truck's out front." He opened the front door. "I can wait while you get your things."

As she climbed down the steps, a man darted across the street. Another man jumped out from behind his truck, parked at the curb.

Faith gasped.

Gabe stepped in front of her. "What—?"

A bright light blinded him. Dots and fuzzy circles blurred his vision. "Faith?"

She shoved him. "Get inside now."

He couldn't see, let alone move. Someone pulled at

his arm dragging him backward. Faith. He didn't want anyone to hurt her. If only he could see…

"Come on, Gabriel," she said, her voice impatient. "Move it."

He stumbled on the steps, but didn't fall. Inside, he had to get her inside.

"What's your name?" a man yelled. "How well do you know Faith Starr?"

"Are you fiancé number six?" another man shouted. "Have you set a date?"

The rapid-fire questions made him dizzy. He couldn't keep all the words straight. As his vision cleared, he blinked and saw a wave of cameras, microphones and people surging up the walkway toward the porch steps.

Oh, man. Gabe turned to the house and nearly collided into Faith as she struggled to open the front door. He covered her hand with his and pushed down so the door latch released. The door opened. Momentum carried them forward into the house. Footsteps pounded behind them. Without a backward glance, he slammed the door and locked it.

Sweat ran down his back, and he gasped for air. He felt as if he'd just run a marathon, not made a quick dash back into the house.

She leaned against the door and slid to the floor. Her shoulders slumped. The color drained from her face.

"Faith?" he asked.

She jumped at the sound of her name. Her reaction disturbed him, sent him into protection mode. Gabe placed his hand on her shoulder and he hated the way she tensed. "Are you hurt?" he asked.

People pounded on the door and called her name. She flinched. "Don't let the piranhas in."

"The who?"

"The press," she said, her tone flat. "I wonder how much they paid to find me."

Reality settled on him—her reality. Did she really deal with this kind of thing all the time? He understood her bitterness. Someone had sold her out. Someone in Berry Patch. Someone they probably knew.

"Looks like the tile will have to wait," she said. "I'm sorry. I've ruined your plans for the afternoon."

He'd forgotten all about the tile. This was about more than ruined plans, a ruined afternoon. This was her life.

"I need to lock all the doors," he said. "I'll be right back."

She nodded.

As he went to the sunroom, he glanced out a window. People crammed the porch, peered inside and snapped pictures. He sat next to Faith. She'd picked the one place where no one could see her from the outside. Luck or experience?

More likely the latter.

Gabe locked the sunroom door, the dining-room doors and the kitchen door. As he walked back to Faith, he wondered what her life in the spotlight had really been like. If the last two minutes had been any indication, her life hadn't been all drinking champagne and eating bon-bons in her pajamas. He stared at her huddled on the floor. For the first time he realized the difference between Faith Starr and Faith Addison. His heart went out to both of them.

No wonder she'd wanted to escape her old life to the

normalcy and predictability of a small town like Berry Patch. It was the only place she had any privacy. The only place no one wanted something from her.

But that wasn't exactly true.

He wanted something from her, too. And not just one thing. He wanted her house, but he also wanted her. Guilt pressed down on him.

Faith deserved better, especially from him.

Gabe had no experience dealing with this, but he had to do something. He had to help her through this. He sat next to her. "What can I do?"

"Nothing." The word was nothing more than a hushed whisper. Tears brimmed in her eyes. "It's all over."

"They'll go away."

"They don't go away." Her lips thinned. "They never go away. And now everyone will know about the house, follow me around town, treat me differently—"

She choked on a sob.

Helplessness washed over him. He hated this feeling. Give him a hammer or a blueprint or a fistfight on a job site, and he could manage. But now… He hadn't known what to say to Kate when Matt had drowned and with Faith, Gabe was just as clueless.

She buried her face in her hands.

Ah, hell. A vise grip tightened around his heart. He hated seeing her like this. He wanted to comfort her, protect her. "Faith."

"Give me a minute."

Forget that. A second more of this was too long.

Gabe pulled her onto his lap. She stiffened in his arms, but he wasn't about to let her go. He rocked her. Gently. Back and forth. She didn't pull away.

He wanted to bury his hands in her hair, soak up its grapefruit scent and never let go. Instead he smoothed her hair with the palm of his hand. With each stroke, some of her tension evaporated until she sank against him.

Her soft curves molded to him.

Desire coursed through his veins, and Gabe struggled against it. Faith needed a friend, not a lover. Still, he brushed his lips across the top of his head.

She stared up at him through spiked eyelashes. Her lips parted slightly.

All he wanted to do was kiss her and make it all go away, for her sake and his. But he didn't dare. Not now. Not with the media circus on the other side of the door. Not with Faith so upset.

Her gaze held his, and he struggled not to lower his mouth to hers. One taste wouldn't be enough. It would never be enough.

A water buffalo stampede sounded on the stairs and was like a bucket of cold water dumped on him. Faith scooted off his lap.

Bernie was the first one down. As she stared out the window, her mouth gaped. "What—?"

"Get away from the windows," Gabe yelled.

She ducked and crawled toward him and Faith. J.T. and Eddie did the same.

"Where did they all come from?" J.T. asked. "The entire street is jammed with cars and those vans with satellite dishes on top."

Gabe didn't take his eyes off Faith. "They were hiding until we came out."

Eddie nodded "I think *Extra!* is here."

"I'm calling 911." Bernie pulled out her cell phone from a pocket, but before she could dial a siren sounded. "Looks like they're on their way."

But what good would the Berry Patch sheriff's department be to Faith? Not very much, Gabe realized with a heavy heart. Which meant it was up to him to see Faith got what she needed. He didn't know what to do, but someone else might.

"Call Henry. He'll be able to help." Gabe glanced at J.T. and Eddie. "Cover the windows with newspaper, trash bags, whatever you can find. We'll need No Trespassing signs."

"We're on it, boss." J.T. headed to the kitchen. Eddie followed him.

Faith's hand covered his own. So small, so soft, so strong. Strength and determination returned to her eyes. His respect for her grew.

"Thank you for being here, for doing all this for me."

"You're welcome." Her gratitude clawed at his heart. This wasn't only for her, was it? "Whatever you need. We'll get through this."

Hope glimmered in her eyes. "We?"

He squeezed her hand. "Yes, we."

She blinked, leaned over and kissed him. Hard, fast, perfect. Then she backed away. Gabe stared at her, unable to speak, think or breathe.

Faith smiled softly. "Then *we* had better get busy."

Once again her life was being played in public and the stage was this small town she'd come to think of as a home away from home. Her family, however, didn't want her anywhere but with them.

"I'm doing fine, Mom." Sitting on the small sofa in the carriage house, Faith adjusted the headset to her cell phone. She'd been on the phone with her family as soon as the news broke, but she hadn't been able to alleviate their concerns. She wasn't going to give up trying. "The sheriff has been very understanding and accommodating. He set up a barricade to keep the media and crowds back from the house and is sending patrols by constantly. I'm in no danger here."

Faith glanced at the RV parked a few feet from her door. It had arrived only two hours ago compliments of Henry Davenport. Forget about needing a professional security team, she'd never felt safer, more protected in her life. She stared at Frank, the wonder guard dog, lying in front of her door and tossed him a cookie.

"But you don't need to stay in Berry Patch. You need to be home with us," her mother, Starr Addison, said.

"I need to stay here for the remodel."

"Starr Properties will buy the Larabee Mansion and finish the remodel for you."

"I want to do it myself."

She needed to do it herself.

"Honey." Starr's voice softened. "You have nothing to prove."

That was *so* not true. And now she'd failed. Faith blinked back tears.

"Don't you know, sweetie. Starr Properties has wanted to buy the Larabee Mansion for the past two years."

Faith straightened. "They have?"

"But each time Will approached Olivia Larabee she

said she had a standing offer from a friend of the family. Don't you see, Faith," Starr said. "You succeeded where none of us could by buying the house. I know your brother and father will be impressed."

Pride filled Faith. She hadn't succeeded the way she'd planned, but she hadn't failed, either. She threw Frank another cookie and bit into one herself.

"It's time for you to come home, baby."

Faith wasn't ready to pack her bags just yet. She might have succeeded, but she had more work to do. She stretched out on the couch. "I will be home once this project is completed."

"You sound just like your father. And brother."

See, she was an Addison just like the rest of them. Faith beamed. "Thank you."

"Is there another reason you want to stay?" Starr had worked so hard with her speech therapy after her strokes. She still slurred a few words, but she had come further than the doctors expected. Faith chalked that up to the love her mother shared with her father. "We've heard rumors about a man. Have you met someone new?"

Faith sighed at the concern in her mother's voice. "My contractor."

"Do you think that's such a good idea?"

"I don't know."

A long pause. "What exactly is going on, Faith?"

"I-it's complicated."

Starr blew out a puff of air. "If a man is involved, it always is. I'm getting worried."

"Don't worry. His name is Gabriel Logan." Just saying his name sent a tingle down Faith's spine. She ignored it. Tried, at least. "He's…nice. You would like him. He's doing a great job with the house. He's talented, dependable, responsible and has all these wonderful ideas." She glanced out the window and saw a figure move inside the RV. "He really looks out for me."

"He sounds perfect."

"He does, doesn't he?"

Frank whined, and she tossed him a cookie.

But how could Faith know for sure?

"Don't rush into anything," her mother cautioned.

"I won't." She and Gabriel had been thrown together by chance. Okay, it was actually Henry Davenport not chance, but without the remodeling project they would have never met. And now with the media circus raging around them, things were spiraling out of control. "I've taken chances before and gotten burned."

"Everyone makes mistakes."

"I've made so many mistakes when it comes to men." Faith was nervous, more than a little scared. Yet Gabriel seemed to make things better, and when she kissed him everything seemed…perfect. "What if Gabriel is no different?"

Her mother tsked. "Don't sell yourself short, Faith. Whether Gabriel is the one for you is another story, but don't be afraid to try again. Love is worth the risk."

"I'd settle for like."

Starr laughed. "I guess you do need to stay in Berry Patch and figure out a few things. We'll need to arrange protection for you. Bodyguards, a security detail."

"Henry and Gabriel already took care of that."

"Oh, really?"

"Yes, really." Faith smiled. "There is a sparkling

new RV parked between me and the garage to house my bodyguards. Gabriel and two of his crew decided to stay after the press arrived this morning."

"And they are big."

"And strong," Faith added. "And not only do I have the three musketeers right outside my door, I have a guard dog right inside my door."

A beat passed. "You hate dogs."

"I'm scared of dogs," Faith corrected. "But Frank and I have an understanding. He keeps his distance and I feed him whatever he wants."

"Don't forget, most dogs are allergic to chocolate."

Faith stared at the half-eaten bag of chocolate chip cookies she'd shared with Frank. Most dogs didn't mean all dogs. And it didn't seem to be hurting the big lug. Still she wrapped up the package. "I won't give him chocolate."

Frank moaned.

Sorry, boy, she mouthed.

"Keep us posted."

"I will, Mom."

"And not just about the house."

Faith smiled at her mother's irrepressible optimism. Yet she was oh-so-tempted to listen to Starr's urgings…and the promptings of her own heart.

Something was happening between her and Gabriel that belied logic. Something special she hadn't shared with even her mother. Gabriel Logan had become her one constant, her source of strength. But what she felt went deeper than his support, deeper than his friendship.

And that restored a hope Faith hadn't dared to hold for a long time.

She had given up finding her one true love. Her heart beat faster as she stared out the window at the RV. But maybe, just maybe, her one true love had found her.

Chapter Nine

A police siren wailed as it fought the traffic still swarming the street in front of the Larabee house. A news helicopter hovered overhead. Faith ignored the sounds. After two days of sitting in the carriage house thumbing through fixture catalogs, she was finally back to work. She fired the nail gun into a two-by-four, grateful to have something constructive to do.

She'd allowed the paparazzi to rule her life for too long. No more.

Frank barked and sat up.

Faith gripped the nailer and glanced at the doorway. Gabriel stood with a drink in one hand and a folded newspaper in the other. A warm glow flowed through her. He was the one constant in a maddening world and seeing him filled her with intense pleasure. "Hi." Her voice sounded different, husky.

A smile tugged at his lips. "I've never met anyone more determined in my entire life."

"The work needs to be done." She stared at the closet she'd almost finished. "Should I give myself a raise?"

"That would put us over budget." He handed her a drink with a straw. "How about this instead?"

She set the nail gun on the floor and took a sip—chocolate hazelnut milkshake. "Keep bringing me these and I'll be done in no time."

She expected a chuckle. "Is something wrong?"

With tense lines on his face, he nodded.

A cold knot formed in her stomach. Her mind jumped on what could have upset him so much. The house. The crew. His family. She took a step toward him. "What is it?"

Gabriel unfolded the newspaper—a tabloid, actually.

On the cover of the latest edition of *Weekly Secrets* was a photograph of Gabriel feeding her a bite of cake. The headline read: Practicing For The Wedding? Who Is Faith's 6th Fiancé?

Air whooshed from her lungs. She felt…sucker-punched.

Gabriel grabbed the milkshake from her hand and held on to her arm. "Sit."

She couldn't do anything but stare at the picture.

The pose was cozy, intimate, sexy. Desire filled her gaze, but forget about her wanting a taste of frosting. The picture made it look as if she only wanted Gabriel. And the same could be said of the way he stared at her.

Panic rioted, along with uncertainty and doubts. She'd thought she'd found a safe haven in Berry Patch, but once again she'd been wrong. Faith felt violated, betrayed. "Who did this?"

"I don't know, but I intend to find out."

Her gaze remained glued on the photo. "You would never know I was holding Annelise on my lap."

He pointed to a tuft of hair near the dollhouse's chimney. "You can see a little bit of her ponytail."

But no one would ever guess that belonged to a one-year-old. No doubt that's what the editors of *Weekly Secrets* were counting on. Faith was used to this kind of intrusion into her life, but Gabriel wasn't and that made her feel horrible to have brought him into her nightmare. Some of her boyfriends had enjoyed the publicity that came with dating Faith Starr. Others had exploited it. But Gabriel had never wanted this, never asked for it. He hated that whole side of her life or at least seemed to. She wrapped her arms around her chest. "I'm sorry you got dragged into this."

"Hey." He raised her chin with his finger. "This wasn't your fault."

"But—"

"No buts." He gazed into her eyes. "It's going to be okay."

He was right, even though it felt like the end of the world. Unfortunately she knew this feeling well. "This happens to me all the time, but you're not used to this kind of…intrusion."

"Don't forget I have five sisters." He laughed. "Don't worry about me. I can handle it."

"I know you can handle anything."

He ran the rough pad of his thumb along her jaw and

tingles ran down her spine. "I'm going to find out who did this."

His tone implied he was going to do a lot more than that. She stared at him, feeling a mixture of wonder and respect at the man standing in front of her. He was willing to battle her dragons. How could she have ever doubted him?

"You don't have to." She liked Gabriel wanting to be her protector, but he had shown her she didn't need one. "I can take care of myself."

"I know you can, but I want to."

Niggling doubts crept to the surface. She needed to warn him. "You might not like what you find."

"Let me worry about that." He cupped the side of her face. "I'm going to take care of it, and I'm going to take care of you."

"Your fifteen minutes of fame are over." Gabe tossed the offending tabloid on the desk. "I know you're the one who sold us out, Mother."

"Us?" Veronica raised a finely plucked brow. "Don't you mean Faith?"

"Of course I mean Faith." Everything he did was about her. "She's been hanging on these past few days, but this could push her over the edge." He stared at his mother. "Why? Why would you do this?"

"I only took the picture and composed the e-mail," Veronica said defensively. "Your father hit the send key."

She made it sound as if they had forwarded a joke to friends not sent a picture to a grocery-store tabloid. Gabe brushed his hand through his hair. "What was in this for you?"

Veronica boldly met his gaze. "Faith isn't planning to stay in town forever."

"So that gives you the right to make her life miserable?"

"She's an actress," his mother said. "She's used to this."

"Faith *was* an actress." Gabe had thought she'd want to go back to the spotlight, but now he feared she'd run from the spotlight and leave him behind. "She gave that up."

"The town needs her. You can't buy this kind of publicity."

"But you can cash in on it, right?"

"It's my duty as mayor," his mother explained. "This was for Berry Patch. All those people spending money at the drugstore, the market and the gas station. Not to mention the restaurants in town. Hal is beside himself at what The Vine has brought in. The Burger Basket and the Berry Bistro can't keep up with the customers. It's better than Christmas for our merchants' bottom lines! And I've put Berry Patch on the map."

Everything his mother did was always about something or someone else. She cared more about this town than her own children. He clenched his fist. "And what about me?"

"Oh, honey, your stock is only going to up with this." His mother's eyes twinkled. "You'll be beating the women off with your hammer."

"I'm not talking about that, Mom." He took a deep breath and exhaled slowly. Because she was his mother, he felt as if *he* had betrayed Faith, too.

"You promised me you wouldn't tell anybody."

She looked at her desk. "I'm sorry, Gabe."

"Sorry doesn't cut it, Mom."

He wasn't sure who he was fighting more—his mother or himself. He hadn't been exactly truthful with Faith. At least his mother had the town's best interest at heart. He was in this only for the house.

"Berry Patch might be raking in the money and publicity, but you've turned Faith's life into a living hell." He flipped over the tabloid so he wouldn't have to look at the picture. "I wouldn't be surprised if she leaves town."

Which was exactly what he wanted. Or had wanted. Until now. Tears welled in his mother's eyes. "I want her to leave town."

Angry, confused, he stared at his mother. "I thought you liked her."

"I do like her," Veronica admitted. "But I'm worried about you."

This was the last thing he expected to hear. Gabe sat in the chair opposite his mother's. "Why?"

Veronica motioned to the tabloid. "You're falling for Faith."

"It's just a picture—"

"It's not just the picture. I saw how you stared at her at the party, watched her play with Annelise. You have feelings for her."

It was true, only he hadn't thought anybody could tell.

"Yes, I like her, but she's a client."

"She's a lot more than that," Veronica said. "Faith is a beautiful woman."

An image of her formed in his mind. The way Faith

looked at him made Gabe feel as if he could accomplish anything. Her generous smile encouraged him. The determined set of her chin made him realize she was so much more than the pampered starlet he had first thought.

"She is beautiful." It was pointless to deny his attraction. Might as well get it all out in the open. The truth had been gnawing at him already. "And you think a small-town boy isn't good enough for the movie star."

"Oh, no, Gabe, you've got it all wrong." A soft and loving curve touched his mother's lips. "You're much too good for Faith Starr."

He straightened.

"That's why I'm afraid Faith is going to break your heart just as Lana did."

Gabe had compared them. Both women wanted more. Both women wanted out of Berry Patch. But he'd also seen huge differences between the two. Especially during these past few days... "Faith is not Lana."

"No, honey," his mother said. "She's worse. She's been engaged five times and never made it to 'I do.' What does that say about her?"

Once he'd thought the same things about Faith, but not since he'd watched her, gotten to know her, grown to care about her.

"No, Mom." He battled against the uncertainty creeping in. "She works hard. Faith is dedicated and determined. She never complains."

"Those things may be true, but Faith has made it clear to all of us that she doesn't plan to stay in Berry Patch. She even told you that herself."

The truth twisted around his heart. He couldn't—didn't want—to answer.

"That's why I decided to help her move along a little faster with that e-mail to *Weekly Secrets*." Compassion filled Veronica's eyes. "I may have helped Berry Patch, but I really did this for you, Gabe."

Emotion clogged his throat, burned his eyes. Veronica Logan never acted this motherly. But this was not what he wanted, not at all.

"Can you forgive me?" Her voice broke.

"Yes." Of course he forgave her. She was his mother. He understood she had acted out of fear and love for him.

But could Faith forgive him for putting her in this position? He couldn't tell her what she had come to mean to him. Not now. Not after his mother's betrayal. Not after his own...

The automatic light went on outside the carriage house, but Faith had nothing to worry about. Not with Eddie and J.T. out in the RV and Gabriel and Frank inside with her.

She scooted over on the couch to get closer to Gabriel. "So what did you want to tell me?"

"Let me clean up first." He rose, shoved the wrappers from dinner into a white Burger Basket bag and placed it in the trash. "Do you want dessert or a drink?"

"No, thanks." She patted the seat cushion next to her. "Sit."

He did. Faith didn't like that he'd sat as far away from her as possible. She was getting used to his closeness, to his support. Was that the problem? Was Gabriel tired of being the one who always gave while she always took?

"You seem...tense," she said. "Do you want me to massage your shoulders?"

Faith placed her hand on his shoulder and the muscles bunched beneath her palm.

"Uh, no thanks."

She removed her hand. Okay, this wasn't boding well. "What's wrong?"

He started to speak then stopped himself. His face clouded with uneasiness.

Apprehension flickered through her. "You're beginning to scare me."

"I'm so—I don't want to do that. It's just—" he took a breath, but it didn't seem to help him. "I know who told the media you were in Berry Patch."

Her breath caught in her throat.

"It's the same person who gave the photograph to *Weekly Secrets*," he continued.

Uncomfortable silence fell over the room.

Faith didn't know what to say. She'd guessed it must have been someone at the birthday party. Someone close to Gabriel, a member of his crew or his family. She was used to betrayal and disappointment. Gabe wasn't. It pained Faith to know he must be hurting and it was her fault.

She squeezed his hand, offering what little comfort she could.

"It was my mother," he said finally, his voice raw.

Surprise robbed her of breath. She'd expected Lucy, even sweet-but-misguided Eddie. But not Veronica Logan. Faith inhaled. "Why?"

"She thought it would be good for Berry Patch."

The mayor of a struggling small town would think so. Faith pressed her lips together.

"She didn't mean to hurt you."

"What about you?" Faith stared at him. "Did she consider how this would affect you?"

"Yes, I believe she did." He sighed. "You said you didn't want any more apologies, but I am sorry about this. I don't blame you if you can't forgive me or hate me—"

"I don't hate you." The anguish in his voice tore at Faith's heart. She held his hand. "I could never hate you."

"But my own mother…"

"That's right," Faith said softly. "Your own mother. You aren't responsible for what she did."

He stared at her, his eyes dark and seeking.

"I wish she hadn't done it. Boy, do I ever," Faith admitted. "But she did and we all have to live with it."

"How can you be so levelheaded about this?" Gabriel asked.

"I was once sold out by my own fiancé. Trust me, it could be a lot worse than your mother."

It could have been you.

Faith pushed aside the quick and disturbing thought. That would never happen. She felt it not only in her heart, but deep within her. He had been her rock these past two days. And in coming to her honestly about his mother's part in this media fiasco, Gabriel Logan had proven himself to her tonight. She could trust him. And…she did.

The realization filled her with happiness, made her

feel fully alive for the first time since she couldn't remember when.

"I want to do something," he said with sincerity.

She smiled. "You've done enough."

"No, I haven't." He placed his arm around her. "I want to make this better for you, but I don't know how."

Desire flared, temptation, too. A new sense of strength grew inside her. For once Faith wasn't afraid to give in to it.

She gave him her best sex-kitten look. Funny, it had taken hours working with a top cinematographer to get it right, but staring at Gabriel, it was like second nature.

"I can show you how," she purred. The suggestive glint in Gabriel's eyes sent her confidence spiraling. "But you have to do what I say."

He moved closer to her. "What are you—the puppet master?"

"Think of me as the…director." She smiled. "I want you to face me."

He did. "Like this?"

"Perfect." Her heart pounded. Her fingers ached to touch him. "Now close your eyes."

He did.

"And—" she leaned into him, the anticipation almost unbearable "—action."

She brushed her lips against his, drinking in his sweetness, gentleness, strength. The featherlight kiss drew her closer, made her want more of him. She parted her lips, her eagerness surprising her.

"Cut!" Gabriel said, drawing the kiss to a premature end.

Faith opened her eyes and stared at him, but she didn't back away. "I'm the director."

His breath fanned her face. "Sorry, but your motivation felt off."

"Off?"

"Yes, off." Mischief filled his eyes. "You need to try that again."

A hot ache grew inside her. She wanted another kiss. She needed another kiss. "If I must."

He grinned. "I'll just face you again, close my eyes and…"

"Action," she murmured, her lips already against his, reclaiming her kiss.

His arms encircled her and Faith went willingly onto his lap. He increased the pressure against her lips, sending a shock wave through her entire body. She never wanted the pulsating sensations to end.

He wove his hands though her hair, his touch as intoxicating as his kiss.

Faith parted her lips, half expecting to hear "Cut!" again. But she didn't. She explored, tasted, teased. Her lips burned, but that only made her want more. She wanted all of him.

Her hands splayed on his back. So strong, so solid.

"We should stop," he murmured, not removing his lips from hers. "Before it's too late."

But she didn't want to stop, not ever.

And that's when Faith knew stopping was what she needed to do. She drew back, caught her breath. But even though he no longer kissed her, Faith's lips continued to tingle. It was all she could do not to touch them and prove the kiss had been real.

"Faith…"

The look of desire in his eyes sent a rush of power through her. "Don't you dare apologize."

"I'm not sorry for kissing you." He grinned. "I just want to know when we can start work on the sequel."

"Soon." She smiled back. "Very soon."

Chapter Ten

Sitting in a red vinyl booth at the Berry Bistro, Faith smiled over her lunch menu at Gabriel. "Is this a date?"

He looked startled, then grinned. "Yeah, it is. Do you mind?"

"No." She winked. "It's about time."

And it was. Faith hadn't known what was going on between her and Gabriel these past weeks, but she hadn't minded. Not with his showering her with kisses and attention. Not with the remodeling in the final stages of completion. She had never been happier.

"I want to celebrate," she said.

"Because the press are gone?"

"Yes." Faith reached out and touched his hand resting on the table. "And I have you to thank for sticking by me."

"Don't thank me." He turned his hand over and

clasped hers. "You should thank Rio Rivers for proposing to that pop diva during her live concert and providing a distraction."

"Poor thing." But even the thought of the media circus now plaguing the popular singer couldn't spoil Faith's mood. Not today.

"This is a nice place." Faith looked around the bistro, filled with locals sipping strawberry lemonade, dipping bread in olive oil and exchanging small-town gossip. Each table had a vase of fresh flowers and a candle. The waitresses wore pink skirts, white blouses, lace-trimmed aprons and smiles. "Is this where Henry first met Elisabeth?"

Gabriel nodded. "Until last year, this place was called Kathy's Korner Kafé, but the Berry Bistro sounded more upscale."

"Change is a good thing."

"As long as the berry cobbler remains on the menu, I can handle whatever change Kathy wants to throw at us."

As Faith stared at him, a warm feeling settled in the center of her chest. This was it. He was it. Her one. Each moment she spent with him and even those she didn't told her that. Not to mention those kisses... She picked up her glass of ice water and sipped, but it didn't cool her down.

"Henry told me you got offered a movie deal? Is that another reason to celebrate?"

"*Jupiter Tears* may have gotten rave reviews and become a box-office hit, but I'm not interested in doing movies again."

A beat passed. "You're sure—?"

"Positive." Faith no longer had doubts. About anything. For the first time, everything was clear to her. She was finally…at peace with what she'd done in the past and where she wanted to be in the future. "That's not what I want."

"What do you want?" he asked.

You.

She wanted Gabriel.

Because of him, Faith had started believing in one true love and happily ever after. If only she knew how to get from here to there…

"Gabe?" a decidedly feminine voice asked.

An attractive woman with long blond hair walked toward their table. Her denim miniskirt accentuated the sway of her hips. Her black tank top showed off her breasts. She exuded sensuality. Sex. And her gaze was focused squarely on Gabriel.

Just let her try. Faith squared her shoulders.

He rose from the booth. "Lana."

"I thought it was you." The woman kissed his cheek. "It's been a while."

Faith watched the exchange. Gabriel was friendly, yet maintained his distance.

"Are you still living in Seattle?" he asked.

Lana nodded. "I just got into town yesterday. I'm on my way to San Francisco and stopped by to see my mother for a couple of days."

Gabriel motioned to Faith. "There's someone I'd like you to meet."

Faith smiled.

The woman did a double take. "So there really is a story behind that photo in the tabloid. Good for you two."

The woman seemed genuinely pleased. Faith rose and extended her arm. "I'm Faith Addison."

"Nice to meet you," she said, shaking hands. "Lana Logan."

"A cousin?" Faith asked.

Lana laughed. "No, I'm not Gabe's cousin."

He met Faith's gaze somberly. "Lana is my ex-wife."

Ex-wife. Faith's world shifted on its axis.

That meant Gabriel was divorced.

She stared at him while her mind spun and her stomach churned.

Divorce was a four-letter word in the Addison dictionary. None of her family had ever been divorced. None had ever separated. None of her previous fiancés had ever been divorced. For all her mistakes, Faith had known better than to pin her heart and her hopes on a man who had already lost the marriage sweepstakes.

And now…

Had she just made the biggest mistake of all?

Faith shuddered at the thought.

Somehow she managed to continue talking with Lana even though her brain was no longer functioning—something about *Jupiter Tears*—but Faith couldn't remember what had been said two seconds ago.

She felt an acute sense of loss. Her family believed in one true love and a marriage lasting until death do you part. That's what she believed, too, yet Gabe hadn't.

Where did that leave them? How could he be "the one"?

"Nice meeting you, Faith." Lana kissed Gabriel on the cheek again. "Good luck."

"You, too, Lana," he said. "Drive safely on your way down to San Francisco."

Trust Gabriel to be protective, even of his ex-wife.

He wiped the lipstick marks off his face and sat. "That was…awkward."

"No problem." Faith's voice sounded terse even to her, but she couldn't help it.

"I hope I didn't put you on the spot, introducing you like that."

The old Faith would have mumbled assurances and run. That's what she was tempted to do, but she couldn't pretend he hadn't come to mean a lot to her these past weeks. She couldn't be wrong about him. She just couldn't be.

"No." She tilted her chin. "I wish you would have introduced us sooner."

His forehead creased. "I couldn't have. You heard Lana. She only arrived in town yesterday."

"No, I meant…" What did she mean? "I wish you had told me you were divorced."

He shrugged. "Guys don't really like to go around broadcasting their failures."

"Women don't really like finding out there is an ex-wife by being introduced to them." Faith ignored the urge to toy with her napkin. "This would be a good time for an apology."

"I'm sorry."

She didn't feel better.

"I've tried to put my divorce behind me." He met her gaze. "Lana and I were only eighteen when we got married. Too young to know what we were doing. Too stupid to care. We were divorced less than a year later."

Faith still didn't feel any better. She wanted to un-understand. "Did you try to resolve your differences?"

"No."

"Did you go to counseling to save your marriage?"

"Hell, no. There was nothing worth saving." He leaned forward and lowered his voice. "We should have never gotten married in the first place. That's why divorce was the only option."

"Divorce is never the only option," Faith said. "What about compromise?"

"I know all about compromising, thanks to you." The way Gabriel stared at her made her toes curl—the last reaction she wanted. "All we've done on the house is compromise."

It was true. She thought back to that first day. "Victorian versus craftsman."

"Sage-green paint versus celadon."

A smile tugged at her lips. "Drapes versus blinds in the bathroom."

"Compromising wasn't always easy, but by doing it we created something wonderful together." A muscle ticked at his jaw. "With my marriage, it wasn't like that. I had this idea of the perfect life and pulled Lana into it, never asking what she wanted out of life herself. I dreamed of forever and ended up divorced at nineteen."

"So you believe marriage can be forever?" Faith held her breath waiting for his answer.

"I do."

She released a sigh. "So do I."

And she knew with abrupt clarity. She hadn't been

wrong about Gabriel Logan. Divorced or not, he was
the one for her. Now all she had to do was find the perfect time to tell him…

Gabe had been waiting for the right time to ask Faith
to stay in Berry Patch, but each time something or
someone had interrupted him. He wasn't going to let
that happen again. The house was finished. She would
be making plans to leave soon. It was today or never.

"It's perfect." She clapped her hands together. "Absolutely perfect."

She was the perfect one.

He had it all planned out. He would propose at the
foot of the tree where they'd first met, they could marry
in Lake Tahoe since Faith's mother didn't like to travel
and have a reception here in Berry Patch after their honeymoon. They would live in the house with Frank and
start a family in about a year or so.

They would be the perfect family living the perfect
life in the perfect house in the perfect town.

She ran from room to room, her excitement conta-
gious. "Will is going to flip when he sees this place."

"Your brother? He's coming here?"

She nodded. "My brother and my father."

Gabe grinned. Maybe he'd have the chance to ask
for her hand in style. "Why?"

"For the walk-through." She hugged herself. "I can't
wait to show them the Gables Inn."

His smile faded. "You mean…"

"That's what I want to call it." She beamed. "Isn't
it perfect? It will be the crown jewel of Starr Properties. At least their B and B division."

Her words sank in. Something wasn't quite right, but he didn't understand. "Starr Properties belongs to your family."

"Yes."

"But the house belongs to you."

"Not for long." She glanced around the room with a wistful expression. "I'm selling it to them."

He staggered. "Why?"

"That's been my plan all along." She ran her hand along the wood banister. "Though I will miss this old house. I've come to think of her as home." Faith sighed. "But she'll be a wonderful addition to Starr Properties' portfolio. And I can always stay here when I come back to check the property with my new job."

Gabe struggled to understand. The house. He had never had a chance at it. He would never own it. He would never live in it. His dream was…dead.

And the woman who had killed it couldn't wait to leave town. And start her new job.

Faith bubbled with happiness and excitement. "Did you know my family has been trying to buy this house from Miss Larabee for years, but she always told them she had a standing offer from a family friend until I came around."

"She did have an offer." His voice hardened. "Mine."

Faith's eyes widened. "What?"

"Ever since I was a boy I have dreamed about owning this house," he explained. "Miss Larabee promised to sell me the house until you made her an offer she couldn't refuse."

As Faith's face paled, her forehead wrinkled.

"I had no idea," she said. "Why didn't you tell me?"

Tell her? His actions had spoken louder than words. During the demolition stage when he had carefully removed all of the moldings and trim so no piece would get broken. During the framing when he made sure the new suites fit the overall plan of the house without ruining its integrity. During the finishing stage when he put his heart and soul into restoring the Larabee Mansion to its formal glory.

She should have seen every bit of love he showed the house. She should have seen every bit of love he showed her. If she truly cared about him, she would have seen it. But she didn't and she hadn't.

The knowledge seared his heart, threatened to bring him to his knees. But he remained standing, remained steadfast. She would not bring him down.

There was only one thing left for him to do. Erect a wall around his heart so she wouldn't be able to hurt him again.

"Why?" she asked again.

"Henry told me you were going to sell the house when you finished remodeling it, so I thought I could buy it from you when you were ready to leave Berry Patch."

"When I left," she mumbled. "This entire time you thought you could buy the house from me?"

Gabe nodded. "The house meant more to me than anything."

"I see." A chill hung on the edge of her words.

"Do you?" he asked. "Do you really see, Faith? This house isn't meant for a B and B, for strangers to enjoy. It's meant for a family. For a husband and wife to raise a family."

"A family," she said.

Gabe realized that he'd only been kidding himself. If Faith had wanted to stay in Berry Patch she would never have offered to sell her family this house. She didn't want him, didn't want the house they had worked on together. He'd been dreaming, fooling himself.

He looked her straight in the eye. "My family."

She flinched. "So everything—you and me—has been about the house."

"Yes. No. Maybe." Gabe brushed his hand through his hair. He didn't want to hurt her. Not the way she had hurt him. "It started out that way, but then it changed."

"And now?"

"I don't know." He couldn't see past the death of his dream, but at least he could rescue his pride. "You never planned on staying in Berry Patch."

"I didn't."

Her words struck like a spear trying to pierce the barrier around his heart. "You wanted to sell the B and B to your family."

"I did."

The spear breached his hastily constructed wall. "You wanted to work for them."

"Yes."

Bull's-eye. His heart split wide-open. He'd never had a chance at the house or with Faith.

"Then you have everything you ever wanted, don't you?" he asked bitterly and left.

"Are you sure this is what you want to do, Faith?" Her father Bill asked.

She wasn't sure of anything anymore.

Sunlight streamed through the carriage-house window, but Faith shivered. Everything she'd come to believe, hope for, want was gone. Her heart, once buoyant and overflowing, was deflated and empty. Maybe once she was home she could forget, at least pretend to forget, and heal her shattered heart. Until then…

"Yes, I'm sure." She slid her last suitcase from the closet and opened it on the bed. "There's no reason for me to stay here any longer."

"Good, because we're all so happy you're coming home where you belong," Will said. "Your future niece or nephew needs an auntie to baby-sit her or him."

They both were so happy, and all she wanted to do was cry. She forced the corners of her mouth up. "I can't wait."

And she couldn't. But her return would be bittersweet. She wished it was her own family she was going home to—a husband, kids, a giant dog named Frank.

Tears welled. She blinked them away.

"You okay, sis?" Will asked.

"I'm…" She glanced out the window at the house, a house he wanted more than her, and closed her eyes for a moment. "I'll be fine once I'm back home where I belong."

Away from here, the house, Gabriel.

Her father handed her a pair of jeans. "It can be hard letting go of something you put your heart into."

He had no idea.

It wasn't the house—though the remodel had gone beyond her wildest expectations and turned the Larabee Mansion into a Craftsman masterpiece. It was Gabriel. That was where her heart lay. With him.

But Faith had no choice. She folded the jeans and placed them into the suitcase. "It's what I've been working toward."

Only she'd forgotten her end goal and gotten distracted. Once again she'd picked the wrong man. A mistake, yes, but it could have been worse.

Though she couldn't imagine feeling any worse than she already did.

Tears stung her eyes again, but Faith was not going to cry. Gabriel Logan was no different from most of the other people in her life who wanted something from her. He didn't deserve her tears.

How could she allow this to happen? How could she have made the same mistake again?

Because she'd wanted to believe, Faith realized. She'd let this happen. She needed to take responsibility.

Gabriel had never told her "I love you." He had never proposed marriage. He had never made plans for their future. But he had showed her what she wanted, what was possible. Maybe she wasn't the best judge of men, but that didn't mean she had to spend the rest of her life alone. Somewhere out there had to be the one for her. And if her aching heart ever got over Gabriel Logan, she would find him.

"It's natural to be having second thoughts," Will said.

"Your brother's right," her father said. "Letting go isn't easy, which is why we have a string of properties. Your mom never could stand to part with any of them."

Faith closed her suitcase. "Well, I'm ready."

Will picked up the suitcase from the bed. "I'll take it to the car."

"Thanks," she said.

Her father's eyes clouded with concern. "We want the Larabee house, sweetheart, but the decision is yours to make. No matter what you decide, you have a position and an office waiting for you at Starr Properties."

"Thanks, Dad," Faith said quietly, wishing she could quiet the tumble of thoughts rumbling through her head. "Would you mind waiting a few minutes? There's something I have to do."

"Take your time, honey." He picked up a duffel bag from the floor. "That's one of the advantages of having a corporate jet. We never miss a flight."

Sitting on the front porch of the Larabee house, Gabe patted Frank. "This is it, boy."

The dog groaned and rolled onto his back.

"I know how you feel." Gabe pulled the house key from his pocket and stared at it. So many years of trying to make his dreams a reality came to an end today. He tossed the key into the air and caught it. If only he could hold on to his dream as easily. "But we'll get over it."

Over her.

With disbelief in his eyes, Frank stared up at him.

"We will get over this," Gabe said for both their sakes. "It's just a house. And Faith is just…"

A beautiful, intelligent, one-in-a-million woman.

One who wasn't going to stay in Berry Patch, Oregon. And one who didn't want him. He ignored the ache inside.

Frank sat up, his large ears lopping against his head.

"What is it?" Gabe asked.

The dog panted.

Faith strolled up the walkway. "Hi."

Gabe straightened.

She scratched behind Frank's ears. The dog stared up at her in total adoration. Gabe felt a twinge of jealousy. Over a dog. Now that was stupid.

"I'll miss you, Frank," she said.

And that's when it hit Gabe. This was goodbye. To the house. To his dream. To Faith. He rubbed his fingertips over the jagged edge of the house key for the last time.

He handed her the key, but she didn't take it. Instead, she shoved her hands into her jeans pocket. "Keep it."

A million and one reasons for her words ran through his mind. "Why would I need a key to the house? All the work is done. Even the walk-through."

"I want to—"

Stay. His pulse quickened.

"Sell you the house."

The air whooshed from his lungs. "What did you say?"

"I want to sell you the house." Her gaze met his. "That is, if you still want it? Do you want it?"

"Yes, but what about selling it to your family?"

"I, uh, I haven't told them yet."

Gabe stared at her. "Selling the house to Starr Properties was the entire reason you bought the house."

She shrugged. "The house is meant for a family, not strangers."

"Are you sure?"

"Do you want the house or not?" she asked, impatience lacing each of the words.

"Yes."

She didn't miss a beat. "Now you can be the one with everything you ever wanted. A real estate attorney will handle the transaction since I'll be...gone. I'm flying home with Will and my dad today."

Overwhelmed, Gabe brushed his hand through his hair. Faith was handing him his dream. He had the dog. He had the house. All that was missing was...the wife.

His heart filled with surprising warmth looking at Faith. Beautiful, smart, determined. But she didn't want him, didn't want to stay in Berry Patch. A swift pain squeezed his already aching heart. "I don't know what else to say except thanks."

"You're welcome."

"Would you like to do the walk-through now?" Gabe asked.

"There's no need," she said. "It's your house. Or will be soon enough."

His chest tightened even more until he thought it would burst. "Will you be coming back?"

"No."

For having just achieved the home of his dream, his victory felt hollow.

"You did a lovely job on the house," she said. "Thank you."

"Thank you."

She started to speak then stopped herself. "I guess this is it."

Tell her to stay. That was the last thing he should do. "Guess so."

She kissed the top of Frank's head. "Enjoy your new house."

"I will." This was it. Say something. Anything. "I hope you find everything you're looking for at Starr Properties."

Her mouth tightened. "Me, too."

He realized they were still holding hands and pulled his away. "Goodbye, Faith Addison."

Her eyes softened. "Goodbye, Gabriel Logan."

Chapter Eleven

The full moon glowed through the branches of the trees and in the mists rising from the floor of the forest. She could hear hooves trampling ahead of her.

Wait. She called out to him. Please wait.

No reply, but his steed had stopped.

The woods were dark, so very dark. She picked up her heavy skirts and ran across the path. Her breath came fast. Pebbles bit through her soft slippers.

As she rounded the bend, she saw him astride a magnificent stallion. The mists of the forest at midnight surrounded them, making both man and beast look larger than life.

I am lost and cannot find my way home.

At your service, milady.

His voice warmed her, filled her heart with hope.

Let me see your face, brave knight, so I may know to whom I entrust my safety.

His gauntleted hand raised the visor fully.

A soft gasp escaped her lips. You. It is you.

The knight smiled. Yes, milady, it is I.

And she knew in her heart she had found him—her one true love—and that he would lead her home.

The knock at the door woke Faith. Dazed, she raised her head from her desk. Even in her dreams she couldn't escape Gabriel Logan. Another knock. She rubbed her tired eyes. "Come in."

Her father entered holding a manila folder in his hand, concern in his eyes. "What time did you get home last night?"

"I didn't. I fell asleep here."

"You need more rest, sweetheart."

She needed to keep busy, to keep her mind off Berry Patch and Gabriel. "I'll rest later. There are two other offers on that inn on the Olympic Peninsula in Washington state, but Will thinks we'll get it with this latest counter. Wait until you see it, Dad. It's been in the same family for four generations. The bones are good. It just needs some updating."

"Sounds good." He smiled his approval. "You've really caught on to all of this."

She nodded, pleased he'd noticed.

"But are you happy?"

"Happy? Of course," she answered quickly. She no longer cried herself to sleep. She no longer craved chocolate hazelnut milkshakes. She'd learned to survive without long, drawn-out kisses. See, happy. "It's wonderful being home and this job is exactly what I thought it would be. Why?"

"You don't seem quite yourself," he said. "Both your mother and I have noticed it."

"I'm still adjusting." Healing. Hoping… No, she wasn't hoping. She was surviving. "That's all."

"I wanted to show you something." He removed a paper from the folder and handed it to Faith. "You drew this when you were little."

She stared at the picture. It was a house. The words *Faith's Three Gables Inn, A Starr Property* were scribbled in crayon at the bottom. "When I saw pictures of the Larabee Mansion, I couldn't help but notice the resemblance."

She took a closer look at the drawing—three gables, a porch and a yellow dog. Not quite a mastiff like Frank. And the scene wouldn't be complete without Gabriel in there somewhere.

Her chest tightened.

"Your mother and I only want you to be happy, Faith," Bill explained, with that wonderful concern still in his eyes. "Perhaps we put too much pressure on you to come home."

"I came home myself."

"We want you to stay, Faith, make no mistake about that, but if you'd rather make movies or—" he cleared his throat "—return to Berry Patch. That's fine, too."

"Berry Patch?"

"Isn't there someone waiting for you?"

"There's no one." No one she could have, anyway.

"Not according to your mother."

"Mom's wrong."

"Are you sure about that?" he asked.

Faith hesitated. "Even Mom can make a mistake."

And so had she. Oh, so had she.

"I should have punched him when I had the chance," her father muttered.

"Dad…" she touched his arm. "This isn't Gabriel's fault."

"Sure it is. He let you down."

"No, he didn't."

And he hadn't.

All Gabriel had done was be himself and give himself. To the house and to her. So what if he'd wanted the house from her? Faith had wanted something from him, too. A guarantee, proof she wasn't making another mistake by falling for him. She hadn't considered Gabriel's wants and needs, only her own.

Regrets assailed her.

Faith thought she'd learned her lesson before, but she hadn't. She hadn't wanted to make a mistake, but she had. She'd made the biggest mistake yet.

Her father grunted, plainly unconvinced.

She trusted his judgment. She always had. But maybe it was time to trust herself. To trust her heart and take a chance on love.

Staring at the picture, her heart filled with longing. A happily ever after was out there waiting for her. She felt it in her bones. She could wait for her knight to find her, or, Faith smiled, she could rescue him herself.

Living in the Larabee Mansion was a dream come true for Gabe. As he walked through the living room, he straightened a throw on the back of his couch. The wool Pendleton blanket had been a housewarming gift from Elisabeth and Henry. A nice touch to Gabe's new home.

His home.

Instead of starting over, he was back on track with his blueprint for the perfect life. The house, the dog...

He stared at Frank lying in front of the fireplace.

He imagined stockings hanging from the mantel and a big noble fir Christmas tree in front of the window. It was all coming together.

Or it would be if he kept telling himself that over and over again.

Who was he kidding? It wasn't coming together. Not without Faith here.

The house was empty. So was his life and his heart.

He plopped onto the couch and stared at the ceiling.

How could he have been so stupid?

All this time he'd been chasing the wrong dream. His father might not have had a plan, but Gabe had clung to his when he should have let it go. Instead, he'd let Faith go.

Idiot.

Frank barked.

Gabe couldn't create the perfect life or the perfect wife. He'd wanted guarantees. He'd ended up with nothing.

Damn. He brushed his hand through his hair. He needed Faith, nothing else. Not even this house.

She was his dream, but he'd been too blind to see it before.

No longer.

He would do whatever it took to be a part of her life. Go wherever he had to go.

"Come on, Frank," Gabe said. "We need to pack."

She'd come home.

As Faith stared at the house—now Gabe's house—she mentally ran through the words she wanted to say. If only she had a script to follow, but no screenwriter was available to help her. No director to stage the scene and make sure it all came together the way it should. She was on her own.

Trusting herself and her heart was the biggest step she'd ever taken. She was terrified.

Be brave.

The front door opened, and Faith's heart lodged in her throat. She mustered her strength, dug deep for enough courage to hold her ground.

Frank lumbered out. He saw her, barked once and trotted down the stairs.

"Hello, there." She knelt to greet the dog. He knocked her onto her bottom. She hugged the gentle giant. "I missed you, too."

"Frank."

The sound of Gabe's voice sent a shiver of anticipation down Faith's spine. Everything she'd been waiting for came down to this. She took a deep breath.

"Faith?" Disbelief sounded in his voice. "What are you doing here?"

She tilted her chin. "Looking for you."

Gabe looked dumbstruck. Great. He wasn't expecting her. He didn't want her. Faith's heart sank to her shoes, but she didn't run.

She glanced at the porch. Something was different.

"You hung a swing." With Frank at her side, she climbed the stairs and sat on the swing. "It's nice."

Gabe sat next to her. "Yeah. Thanks. You were looking for me?"

"I wanted—no, needed to see you again." She stared at the tree where they had first met.

"Well, that's—" he laughed and ran his hand through his hair. "Frank and I were packing when you drove up. We needed—I needed to see you, too."

Her heart beat faster. "Why?"

"I know you hate apologies," he said. "But I wanted to say I'm sorry."

Faith didn't want his apologies. She wanted his love. "You haven't done anything to apologize for."

"Yeah, I have." He blew out a puff of air. "I should have told you about wanting the house."

He should have. She nodded.

"I should have told you the real reason my mom told the press about you was to force you to leave town."

"Why?"

He turned and looked at her with his deep, dark blue eyes and Faith's heart skipped a beat. "My mother was afraid you would break my heart."

The truth washed over Faith; her breath caught in her throat. She realized what his mother's actions would have meant to Gabe, and just how difficult this must have been for him.

"Did I—" Faith stared into his eyes "—break your heart?"

"I did it to myself," he admitted. "You helped me find my heart."

The tenderness of his gaze blanketed her with warmth.

"I've spent years chasing my dreams only to discover they were the wrong dreams. You're what I want, Faith, what I need."

Her spirits soared. "I'm all yours."

His mouth met hers in a possessive kiss. This was where Faith belonged. She had no doubts, no uncertainties.

"Yes, you are," he said. "Off-camera, but I don't mind sharing you on-camera."

She eyed him warily. "Excuse me?"

"I had an idea," he explained, holding her hand. "Home improvement shows are popular. We could take what we both like to do and do a remodeling show together."

She loved the idea. "You'd have to leave Berry Patch to do that."

"Being with you is more important than any town." He squeezed her hand. "And we'll always have this house to come back to when we need a place to call home and raise our children—I mean, sons."

Joy overflowed from her heart. "And daughters."

He cupped her face, and his smile softened. "I love you, Faith."

"I love you, too." She blinked back tears of happiness. "Will you marry me?"

His grin deepened the lines at the corners of his eyes. "Isn't that supposed to be my line?"

"I haven't had much luck the other way around. I thought I'd try something different."

He laughed, a rich, warm sound she wanted to hear each day for the rest of her life. "Different is good."

"Does that mean the answer is yes?" she asked.

"The answer is yes," he said. "But does that mean people are going to start calling me Mr. Faith Starr?"

"Actually it's Mr. Faith Addison, but I'll settle for Mrs. Gabe Logan."

He caressed her cheek. "I like the sound of that."

"Me, too." She sighed, realizing there was only one thing she wasn't looking forward to. "But…can we skip all the wedding stuff?"

"What wedding stuff are you talking about?"

"Not the ceremony, but everything else. I really want to marry you, but I don't want to plan another wedding."

He raised a brow. "What did you have in mind?"

She bit her lip, hoping he wouldn't mind. "Could we…elope?"

"The truck's gassed up and my bags are packed." Gabe stood and extended his hand. "Let's go now."

"The truck's great, but I have a jet." She grabbed hold of his hand and rose. "We can get there faster."

"Even better."

Frank barked.

Gabe's smiled widened. "Sounds like he already prefers the jet to the truck."

"Smart dog."

"No kidding." Gabe pulled her into his arms and kissed her again. "He found you."

* * * * *

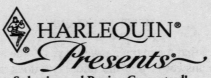

HARLEQUIN®
Presents

Seduction and Passion Guaranteed!

Legally wed, but he's never said…
"I love you."

They're…

Wedlocked!

**The series
in which
marriages are
made in haste…
and love
comes later…**

**Look out for more Wedlocked! marriage stories
in Harlequin Presents throughout 2005.**

Coming in May:
THE DISOBEDIENT BRIDE
by Helen Bianchin
#2463

Coming in June:
THE MORETTI MARRIAGE
by Catherine Spencer
#2474

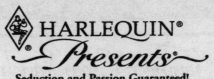

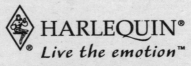

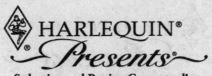

HARLEQUIN®
Presents®

Seduction and Passion Guaranteed!

Introducing a brand-new trilogy by

Sharon Kendrick

THE ROYAL HOUSE OF CACCIATORE

Passion, power & privilege – the dynasty continues
with these handsome princes...

Welcome to Mardivino—a beautiful and wealthy
Mediterranean island principality, with a prestigious
and glamorous royal family. There are three
Cacciatore princes—Nicolo, Guido and
the eldest, the heir, Gianferro.

Next month (May 05), meet Nico in

THE MEDITERRANEAN
PRINCE'S PASSION #2466

Coming in June: Guido's story, in

THE PRINCE'S LOVE-CHILD #2472

Coming soon: Gianferro's story in

THE FUTURE KING'S BRIDE

Only from Harlequin Presents

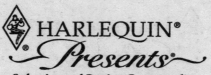

HARLEQUIN®
Presents
Seduction and Passion Guaranteed!

GREEK TYCOONS

**They're the men who have everything—
except brides...**

Wealth, power, charm—what else could a
heart-stoppingly handsome tycoon need?
In the GREEK TYCOONS miniseries you have
already been introduced to some gorgeous Greek
multimillionaires who are in need of wives.

**Now it's the turn of favorite Presents
author Lucy Monroe,
with her attention-grabbing romance**

THE GREEK'S INNOCENT VIRGIN
Coming in May
#2464